SHADOWS

of

SILENCE

Shadows

of

Silence

Heather Roselle

Also by Heather Roselle

Fitness is a Feeling

Surrendering to Possibilities: Life, Yoga & Business

To women who overcome

adversity and discover

their personal strength.

Silence...

a friend who will never obey.

CONFUCIUS

I crouched beside *a fence separating our property from his. Night Star never disappointed me. Appearing as if out of thin air, his welcoming hand slid into mine. Pure joy. Our plans were in motion.*

Lifting me onto his horse, he slipped on behind me.

I could smell the water before I saw it, the moon gloriously reflecting its image for the universe to admire. We both slid off, checking to ensure we were alone.

Sheltering under a tree, Night Star paused. "The moon bath must first connect with our skin."

With that, he lifted the layers of clothing from his body and stood before me naked.

There was only one word to describe what I saw: exquisite. This was the first time I was to gaze upon a boy very obviously on the verge of becoming a man.

I, in turn, awkwardly tried to remove my boots. Struggling until common sense suggested I sit first, I removed the remaining layers effortlessly. Following his lead, I stood before him naked; naked for the first time with someone other than my own company or the company of my nanny.

It felt natural.

Innocent and pure.

He was my friend and I was his.

Based on his comfort with me being on the verge of womanhood, I suspected my naked body was not the first he had seen.

Again, he slid his hand in mind, "Now, we follow the invitation of the waves touching the shore."

The water was warm, making it easy to wade deeper into the water until only our shoulders and heads remained above.

"Ready?"

I nodded, we both took in a deep breath and submerged ourselves, our eyes open so we could see each other and the moon above.

Our plan was to see who could hold their breath and stay under the longest, but a gunshot, muffled by water, interrupted the challenge.

Night Star's head was already above mine; something on the shore stilled him.

When I surfaced, I recognized the reason for his rigidity.

Standing in the night's shadows were three male figures—all with guns, all looking our way.

We looked from each other to the opposite shore, and then to the edge from which we had entered.

Sensing what we were thinking, one of them spoke, "I see two choices: out of the water or dead in the water."

Another of the men thought this was hysterical, his laugher as menacing as the choice presented.

Night Star took my hand in his.

A Life for a Life

ALL LIVING THINGS experience urges: to breathe, to eat, to sleep.

I seldom breathed, ate or slept based on urges—these I did to survive. While surfacing less frequently, the urge to kill still appeared unexpectedly.

Tormented souls live tormented lives.

How many times had I wondered if killing would end my torment? Today might be the day to discover.

Stretched before me on my grandfather's well-worn chair was a stranger. Although we'd never met, his being reminded me of others like him; confidently arrogant in the ways of men. The boots furthest from me were crafted with fine imported leather. The trousers and vest, slightly soiled from travel, not labor, were made by hands spanning the distance of an easterly ocean. The face, weathered and tanned, was covered with enough facial hair to be considered a beard.

Relaxed, assuming to be in the hands of an expert, he closed his eyes. At this moment of surrender, I knew my life was not in my hands.

His was.

Reaching across for a moist towel, the inside of my wrist brushed his chin, sensing its coarseness. My right cheek involuntarily stung. Certain of its redness, I glanced at my reflection in the mirror to my right. Though still stinging from a memory, there were no physical signs of redness or irritation.

As my heartbeat increased, his breath became slower, rhythmical and relaxed.

The tools, all left in orderly fashion, awaited. I squeezed the excess water from the towel, welcoming the cleansing of my palms as a personal ritual of sterilization. When the towel touched his face, his breathing paused before continuing with increased peace.

Lifting the polished handle, I tested the suppleness of the bristles. Although each strand was from the same creature, the color variances of charcoal, chestnut and hazel always made me wonder. But this brush was my creation; I knew from which animal these bristles originated.

I moistened the brush then meticulously swirled the brush with soap, inhaling the fragrance. This was the reason so many men stopped here; Paul's shaving soap was an original recipe, adapted from the previous owners of the property, blended to perfection with reserved animal fat, wood ash and dried lilac petals from last spring.

I gingerly lifted the towel and began to blanket his neck, jawline and face with shaving soap. Oddly, with his facial hair veiled by soap, the burning of my cheek ceased.

The process usually lasted longer to ensure the skin was prepared for the razor's edge, but I sought perfection of a different nature; today time was not on my side. Brush and soap set aside, I pressed the straight edge against my palm, teasing my skin's surface to test the presence of blood beneath. But it was not my blood I wished to see today. It was his.

Pressing the blade to his neck, I scraped lather and stubble with a smooth upward pass. Dipping the whitened blade into the basin, I watched the freshly exposed skin pulse with the beating of his heart. Again, I made another line of un-lathered skin, still watching the steady rhythm of his heart. I continued until a single strip of lather remained. Hidden beneath the pureness of this final line of soap was his blood river. My blade rested at the base of the stream.

I was close, but I wanted perfection.

And I wanted to remember.

Gripping the handle tighter, I slowly pulled the blade towards his chin, stopping at the strongest marker of his beating heart. He sensed a change, opened his eyes and I silently bid him farewell. As I shifted to slice rather than strip, a warm larger hand slid under mine.

Using his hip, Paul nudged me from the stool while prying the blade from my hand.

Then, as if this is something we did every day, he asked, "Did you find my list?"

Stunned by his stealth and timing, I clumsily stepped backward toward the list we started earlier this morning.

"He closes in ten minutes," he cautioned, nodding towards the door. Now commanding me to leave, he finished the last section of shaving and, with a fresh towel, covered the stranger's face to protect my identity. "Don't forget the dress code."

Despite knowing what I nearly did, he smiled that sly smile, remembering how much his dear friend loved to see me wearing that apron over what we call my personal uniform.

"You know he'd let me in without it," I said, knowing I had no negotiating power, but that never stopped me from trying.

"Sure he would. When he's six feet under. And that is not today," he said.

No further negotiations would be entertained; I was dismissed. How such a large man could say so little yet command so much continually surprised me. Today these traits saved me from myself.

Loathing the very sight of the apron, not the woman who created and wore it, I slung it around my shoulders so it draped over my back. Once tied, it resembled a cape, sure to raise more than a few eyebrows.

Stepping out the back door, I took a deep breath. My grandfather's property, no matter the season, was as immaculate as his shop.

"Without order there is nothing but chaos," he reminded me each time I was assigned what I perceived to be a menial task. But I did as I was asked, because I knew his wisdom to be true; truth being a rare commodity in my experience.

His property, now measuring 6400 acres, was picturesquely located on the eastern edge of the foothills. Because the main street leading to and from Turner Creek was north-south, the only traffic towards his property was those in need of a haircut, shave or legal advice. Although well respected as a lawyer, he'd sooner be barbering or investigating the next lucrative enterprise. While he loved to be busy, I longed for those rare days without business.

The view from the back verandah was like looking through a camera viewer, creating a unique image every time I stopped to notice. Facing west, I never tired of gazing at the distant Rocky Mountains, especially on a day like today; less snow and more mountain teased the arrival of a long-awaited summer. Soon, I'd be able to leave for weeks on end, losing myself in the solitude of the mountains, thinking of anything except the past and the future.

A steady, familiar plodding nudged me back to reality. Snuffling my pockets was my only true friend, Jack. Too big for most to handle and much too smart for his own good, he was traded for legal services a year ago. I scratched his ears, but the snuffling persisted. Reaching deep into my pockets, I offered a small handful of dried oats excluded from this morning's breakfast preparations.

If I walked to Earl's, I'd be too late. Given Paul's timely arrival before I slit a stranger's throat, I needed to do this one thing for him. He was my grandfather, but he put up with much more than he should.

My tack was easily stored and readily accessed, requiring very little space. I lifted my saddle blanket from the post and draped it over Jack's back. My saddle blanket was fashioned like one created by a dear friend. Embroidered corner star patterns outlined in black were a reminder of his ever-present spirit; one which comforted and haunted me in equal parts. Sliding the blanket over Jack's back was easy; he was a working ranch horse before becoming mine and, compared to the rigid western saddle, he loved the feel of softened leather against his coat.

Caressing Jack's nose, I slid the halter, simply a thin rope of braided leather, over his lower jaw and around his nose, and then separated the leather reins on each side of his neck. In anticipation, Jack side-stepped closer to the verandah's edge. With no stirrups, I relied on his cooperation; he accepted my respect.

Hoisting myself up, I paused with my belly to his back and waited. Jack steadied, a sign of readiness, before I sat up. Once my body and my intention connected with his, I urged him forward with a slight tensing of my heels. Though he'd prefer not to, he walked off my grandfather's property. Once on the rutted trail leading towards town, I released my control.

Jack's sequence was always the same: trot to warm up, canter to limber up and gallop for the pure love of speed and freedom.

Alone in a Crowd

GALLOPING MUST BE like heaven. If there is one. Closing my eyes, I felt the wind pull my hair free from a leather clasp, my shirttails from my trousers and my apron from my back.

Needing no guidance, Jack slowed to a walk as the trail transformed to a defined road leading to Earl's General Store. Without opening my eyes, I already knew there was a crowd out front.

Men.

Smoking cigars.

Trading stories of self-importance.

When I opened my eyes, my prediction was confirmed; they looked like a murder of crows surveying all who dared enter their privileged space.

Why men feel such a need to stare is beyond my comprehension. My grandfather calls it appraising. I call it rude. Jack stopped, nudging a grey mare from the post closest to the stairs. Sliding from his back, pausing as always to reassure him of my return, my feet touched down.

Sometimes avoiding eye contact avoids conversation. Unless it's the newly appointed mayor.

"Hannah, you are a sight on that horse!" Edward inhaled deeply from his cigar, taking in the full length of my form.

"Edward," I replied, taking in the full length of his frame. "You simply are a sight."

I suppose he might have been considered handsome years ago. In his mind, he still considered that to be true. All his wealth had created a false sense of identity. And confidence.

There was a split second when I recognized how my intensity intimidates even a man like Edward. I was prepared for it. The only way Edward knew how to restore his confidence was to either insult or bully.

"A crazy horse for a crazy rider," Edward said and stood a bit taller.

I knew I should just leave it alone. "Jack's the best ride I've ever had."

The four spectators waited, silently enjoying the banter.

"I told you to come see me about the riding part." His crow counterparts snickered with yet another of Edward's indecent invitations.

"I doubt there's much to learn." I curtsied dramatically. "I'll be sure to let my grandfather know," I added a threat of my own, sidestepping towards the door before the horny bastard could recover from choking on his own cigar smoke.

Earl's store had its own way of welcoming me, especially if my arrival coincided with closing time.

But not today.

With cigar-smoking, rich men came scornful daughters and wives. If they were outside, I knew who'd be inside.

Slipping into the store unnoticed was out of the question.

Returning home empty-handed was not an option.

Pondering my strategy left me open to another comment now festering and sure to be more wicked than his previous.

While I loathed the town's women as much as the men, women's methods of intimidation and humiliation had nothing to do with my sexuality.

I pushed the door open.

As anticipated, a group of girls disguised as women were huddled around a bolt of fabric. Never being fluent in fashion, I wasn't so ignorant as to not recognize fine silk, crimson at that, from a distance.

Assuming I was one of their male escorts, Suzanne wrapped one end of silk around her shoulders and turned with awkward sophistication in my direction.

Gazing demurely downwards, she didn't recognize who I was, but her cohorts did; they stood dumbfounded and silent behind her.

How humorous to find this trio of fashionably elite so ill-equipped in the simple matters of communication.

Suzanne was left to the wolves or in this case, me.

"That bolt was pre-ordered. You best keep those lovely hands off my future wedding gown," I challenged.

Feeling far too full of myself, or maybe releasing a bit of steam from my previous urge suppression, I stepped towards the now fully aware Suzanne. Standing a good two hands taller than her, I tugged the fabric from her shoulders and rewrapped the ends around the bolt.

"Wedding?" Suzanne recovered quicker than I anticipated. Surprise was now replaced by cynicism, but my words surfaced faster.

"You didn't receive your invitation?" I said, watching her response.

Wild animals were easy to deal with on my own; women, or in this case, girls, were not. I scanned the room, "Earl! I asked you to keep my special order special."

"You know my weakness is a beautiful woman," Earl winked playfully at Suzanne, his voice immediately quieting the conflict. Unlike his brother, Edward, Earl was as handsome now as he probably was years ago. Like his brother, he acquired a shrewd sense of business. He casually stepped into the space between Suzanne and me.

"Looks like you'll have to decide which of us is a more valuable customer," Suzanne challenged, now pouting.

"Now, Miss Suzanne, you told me there were three other fabrics worth purchasing, plus you haven't even looked at what is coming this fall." Earl redirected her attention as a mother soothes a fussing baby.

Earl took a long draw from his pipe, then reached under his counter for a hefty catalogue. The trio squealed in simultaneous delight.

"Go on now, take this home and pick the prettiest. By the time you're done dreaming 'bout how much more beautiful you'll be, more fabric will arrive."

Handing over the catalogue like a peace treaty, he guided the trio to and then out the door.

All but Suzanne left. "I best not see you wearing that fabric or I'll rip it off in front of everyone," she threatened.

I could have ignored the challenge as I had no intention of purchasing or wearing it; I must admit, I was amused by the force of her threat.

"To which I'd return the honor, leaving you and me naked in front of the finer citizens of Turner Creek. Who do you think will look more beautiful then?" I asked.

Suzanne's face flushed as the image became crystal clear in her mind. Her sheltered life left her ill-equipped to utter comparable profanity.

Her father, lacking no such fluidity, spoke in her stead, "You will apologize to my daughter. And you will do so now." Edward stood stoically protective beside his only child.

"Or you'll show me how to ride?" I said, knowing I was crossing the line.

This was the most entertainment I'd had in a long while.

Suzanne's outburst of tears broke the deadlock. Opting for an exit with dignity, Edward wrapped his arm around Suzanne's shoulders and ushered her out of the store. The silence of their departure increased my awareness of my own racing heart.

"Wish Paul'd send you out for supplies more often," Earl chuckled, flipping the open sign to closed and locking the door. "Rounds out my day with business not as usual!"

Sliding his hand under my elbow, he led me to an ornate refreshment bar, pulled a bottle of root beer and two shot glasses out.

We took the first cool sips in silence until my guilt took over. "I do apologize; they'll take their business elsewhere."

"Maybe in their minds for a day or two, 'til they realize not only is this store convenient, it also is the most unique," he boasted, touching his glass to mine.

"Wise as you are old, Earl." I touched my glass to his.

He spoke the truth. His store was different. While other merchants in Turner Creek, and Calgary for that matter, offered basic needs and necessities, Earl wanted to create a different place to purchase unique and fashionable items. He envisioned, as the area developed an abundance of wealth, providing a surplus of desirable things—things people wanted but didn't need.

I respected him as much as I did my grandfather. "Earl, why do men and women hate me so?" I asked.

"Are you just curious or do you really want to know?" Earl studied my expression.

"I probably don't want to know, but I am curious," I answered honestly.

"There are two answers to your question. One simple. One complex. Simply, you are the most beautiful woman they have ever seen." He took a slow sip before continuing.

Insults I can take; compliments were quite another matter. I was annoyed by my flushed response and wondered why I asked in the first place.

"Your grandfather has already told you that, but it sounds different coming from me. Relax now, don't even think about bolting out that door. Remember, you asked me the question."

He patted the top of my hand then continued. "That said, women envy your beauty. Not because they aren't beautiful in their own way, but because your beauty has a power. Men see your beauty and wrestle between admiration and desire—you make them uncomfortable because you disregard their gestures." He paused and reconsidered. "No, you repel them and their gestures. That makes them jumpy whenever you're around."

"But I don't care what they think. I really don't want anything to do with them." I shook my head.

"Which leads to a complex answer about the two of them. The women and the men. One does somethin' wrong, the other corrects or lies about it. They protect each other because they want protection in return. You protect yourself as if you need no one, or at least that's what you want us to believe," Earl said.

I could feel my shoulders stiffening. "I don't care what others think or what they believe."

"So you say. So you think. But you do care enough to rile them up," he said, taking a good look at me, knowing what was likely going to happen next.

This conversation was heading in the wrong direction. "I better get back."

"Just one more thing. You aren't afraid of what the rest of us fear, because you know something far worse. Whatever the cause of your hurt, you keep your wounds well disguised."

Damn him.

Damn my grandfather.

I felt like I was suffocating and, much as I hated to admit it, fear of what Earl suggested overrode my better judgement.

Forgetting Paul's list, I bolted for the door, awkwardly pausing to release the lock.

Jack stood at attention, sensing the urgency of my arrival signaled a quick, far from eloquent exit. I transitioned from the top stair to straddling the saddle blanket and pressed my heels against him.

Message received. Jack opened into a full gallop, but I gave him no direction.

I remembered there was a time when I valued friendship and companionship, but these days solitude was my only trusted friend.

NIGHT STAR AND *I had secretly been friends for two years. We met quite by chance, teenagers warned not to stray too far from home: for me, the fences outlining my father's property; for Night Star, the emerging boundaries of land separating his people from mine.*

Oblivious to anything other than my fascination with tracks, especially those I thought belonged to a fox, I noticed the unusual movement of several branches of a small wolf willow shrub in front of me.

I crouched protectively low to the ground and froze.

There was no wind today; the movement was caused by something or someone and I knew my strategy of freezing and crouching was ridiculous—my vibrant purple jacket would easily be spotted from miles away by any idiot.

I hated to admit it, but my actions were showcasing my fear. There was nowhere to hide, nowhere to run and, perhaps worse, I had no idea what or who I was hiding or running from.

When a human head cautiously popped up, I saw this threat to be a boy about my age, admittedly handsome, but equally afraid of me.

We had both heard the embellished stories of mayhem and bloodshed in the name of trading and settlement between those with light skin and those with dark skin.

We both wrestled with the next best step.

I stood.

He stood.

We walked slowly together, me studying the beautiful simplicity of his clothing, him studying the ridiculous complexity of mine. Two teenagers alone. Standing face to face.

He smiled.

I smiled and when I did, he offered me his hand. "We are not supposed to be out here," he whispered.

His welcoming touch gave me confidence to continue, "We are not, but did you see these tracks?" I asked, refocusing on why I was here in the first place.

When he knelt to take a closer look, I noted the length of his braid resting between his shoulder blades. He was already long and lean, likely taller than most his age.

He stood up, laughing, "A fox or one the small dogs that live with us."

I couldn't keep from staring.

He was the most attractive boy I had ever seen, and while I would be accused of inappropriate relations in the future, what I observed was simply what a sister or a friend would notice when looking at her brother or friend.

Beauty could easily be described with a name: Night Star.

His hand reached again for mine and he led me to the bush from where he emerged.

Under the shade, I asked, "Why do you speak English?"

"Because my mother can. Why do you speak English?" he laughed. Answering with such logic made my question seem utterly ridiculous.

I knew the stories of women and men who married into the other race; those who dealt with my father sounded like they despised the arrangement, so I was curious about this version of an interracial family but was distracted by his laughter and the promise of friendship.

He reached to loosen the pins pressing my hair to my scalp. It was sweet release as my hair fell past my shoulders. Moving behind me, he ran his fingers through my hair, marveling at the color so near cream compared to his shade of midnight black. Then, as casually as he took my hand, he divided my hair into three strands and braided my hair in the same fashion as his own, although I knew if I loosened his single braid, the full length of his hair would fall lower than his waist.

He looked at his work with pride. "You look different but still the same."

"I don't know how I look, but it feels like the end of my headache." I smiled, wondering how my mother, who had so helped the first nations when they came to the fort to trade, would have looked after my hair if she were alive.

This moment in time was magical; cool when the temperature was warm, simple when the rules for behavior were complex, comforting when loneliness vanished with the bond of friendship—a friendship that would last far beyond his lifetime.

Shaded Invitation

A DISTANT HOWL RELEASED my mind from the trappings of an all too familiar trance. Only then was I able to notice the new but foreign details surrounding me. Jack, warm and sweaty beneath me, stood motionless. This destination was his choice; the purpose was for my wellbeing.

The coolness of the air was familiar, the inky silhouettes of my beloved mountain range stood nearby. While in the company of these rugged peaks, there was a guarantee of solitude. Civilized, well-dressed men and women avoided evening travel.

My apprehension evaporated. I released the reins and lowered my body to Jack's in silent appreciation.

This treasured friend bore more than his fair share of my burden; how many times had he saved me from losing the tiny shred of sanity I called my own?

Sliding from Jack, my feet on the ground, I released him to enjoy the location as much as I did.

Earl had pushed hard today. On numerous other days, my grandfather pushed me in a different way. Both men wanted to protect me, but both wanted me to set myself free from the burden of what I kept silent.

Then I heard it. The joyous sound of water flowing under the melting ice of a river. Rather than avoid it, I walked towards the sound. With the river now in my view, I recognized this as a wildlife trail that would lead me back to Paul's. Although once a year I chose to relive the details of a night long ago, to remember my weakness and recommit to some form of punishment for the rest of my life, I didn't have the strength for that now.

The moon, although partially shrouded by light cloud, indicated my return home would be much, much later than expected.

While my grandfather would worry for brief moments at a time, he'd come to accept my disappearances as a means of maintaining my sanity.

Picking up Jack's reins, we walked along a trail. Resurfacing after solo journeys was always calculated; I returned at night, sometime between the last customer and my grandfather's predictable bedtime.

I entered from the same door I had exited and slipped into the kitchen. Something was alarmingly different.

Draped over a chair was the bolt of crimson fabric from Earl's. Damn it!

Earl must have stopped by, the two of them likely sharing a whiskey or two, speculating on my whereabouts and trying to estimate the time of my return. I was much later than either of them anticipated as there was no sign of Earl, but the barbering room was still dimly lit.

I prayed it was a forgotten detail as I peered cautiously around the door frame.

Instead of being in a deep sleep, Paul was stretched out on the chair, eyes closed, tools ready, "You've got some unfinished business."

I noted his smile; he was relieved I returned safely, but he had something else on his mind.

"Paul, it's way too late." I knew I sounded as weary as I felt, but I exaggerated my fatigue in the hopes he would feel a bit sorry for me and change his plans.

"How about we do this in the morning," I negotiated. If dramatization wouldn't change his mind, maybe common sense would.

"Why put off today what you don't really want to do tomorrow?" he said.

Another of what he called famous last words.

I had no choice. My frustration quadrupled as he was only too aware of how good my shaving technique was; I had been after all taught by him!

Whatever lesson he had in mind would be delivered on his terms.

Pulling a steaming cloth from the barrel was his favorite part; it was one of his emerging innovations: to create a safe source of heat for the pre-shave water. Not too hot, not too cold.

I lovingly wrapped the towel around his face and decided to begin the conversation. "Did Earl tell you about what happened?"

No comment.

His words were always so well thought out, whatever he had to say would be said when he was ready. And only then.

Lather was next. What struck me was the change in fragrance, he decided to use the last of the lavender he imported last year. The lather was thick enough to cover the unshaved, yet thin enough to not interfere with the sharpness of the blade.

As I glided the razor along the lather, now lightly peppered with my grandfather's whiskers, he broke his silence, "Will you let me know if you decide to move that blade for a different purpose? I have a few things I'd like to say before that happens."

His voice was calm, like he truly would accept a moment of my instability.

"I've done this for you dozens of times. Not once did I or will I consider slicing your throat, then leaving you to bleed to death while I steal your worldly possessions," I said, expressing my affection for him sarcastically.

The edge in my voice made him chuckle, "You are so much like her when you get yourself riled up."

His quiet humor faded like the memory itself. He was becoming more sentimental as he aged, and while I longed for him to tell me more about my mother, he only shared small bits at a time. "The only difference between the two of you is your nocturnal disappearing act. Had she done that when she lived here, I wouldn't have lived long enough to help raise her daughter."

"Had she lived longer, you might not be in a position to raise her daughter," I said, anger singeing my sentimentality.

When he looked at me with that grey blanket of sadness, I cursed myself for being cruel to the one person I cared about.

To distract both of us, I finished the last section and pulled another warm towel to wrap around his face. "I just needed to get away. To sort things out. I always come back."

I expected his usual forgiveness.

Instead he lay silent, his thoughts wrapped tightly behind the warm towel. Lifting his hand, he removed the towel. "I'm always thankful when you return. But your return isn't guaranteed."

"I know how to deal with what's out there," I said, disappointed to rehash an old issue.

"So do creatures of the wild. And men who behave wild like the creatures." He hesitated. "Ones used to taking what they want without asking. Ones who think nothing of taking a life."

"How about those men who assume they have the answers, but never ask the right questions?" I barked back.

We were crossing into new territory. Paul usually didn't push when it came to talking about why I was sent away.

"How about those who remain silent rather than clarify the assumptions?" Paul challenged me.

There was so much more to my story than simple assumptions, but I wasn't anywhere near wanting to clarify after so much time had passed. So I defaulted to being silent.

"There will never be peace within you if you don't face what you need to face." He did have a gentle way of continuing the conversation, no matter how difficult.

"I face it alone," I said, wondering how many times I had defended myself with this line.

"And so it continues to haunt you," Paul said.

"You think going back will make anything better?" I said, hearing my voice amplify. "He's been dead in my mind since he sent me away," I said, my earlier defiance returned.

"You say he's dead in your mind. Uncertain if that's true or not, you don't sleep, you don't settle, you don't live. Whether you live with me or somewhere else. And just like a wild animal, you flee when the truth closes in on you," Paul said, rising from the chair.

He only had a few closing moments before my patient respect for him expired. "It's time to start adding people to your life. You will outlive me and I can't bear the thought of you spending the rest of your life alone," he said.

"If you're talking about what happened at Earl's, those are not people worth adding to anyone's life." I knew that was not what he was talking about, but I squirmed when Paul alluded to his life ending.

"I can't argue with you on that point. But I can impress upon you my other points. All of your future connections are based on what you do with your silence," he continued, now sounding more like a lawyer.

"When I should have spoken, I was sent away. When I should have been protected, I was treated like I was the opposite of innocent—" I had to stop talking, the emotion creeping into my voice was not to be trusted.

"Well, love, there may be one person you might be willing to open up to," he said, walking to the door separating the barber space from his office.

Boots cautiously approached the open door before hesitating.

Terror took over, threatening to render me useless; I wondered if the mystery guest would be my father. How dare he think forgiveness was mine to offer.

A breeze from an open window presented an alternate consideration. I could stand and wait or I could escape. Did that make me a coward for not facing this hesitant guest from my past?

My foot was through the exit before I answered my own question.

This was no act of cowardice.

This was taking control.

Whoever wanted to see me could bloody well wait or go back to where he came from.

Reluctant Reply

MUCH AS I hated to admit it, I was exhausted. The exchanges at Earl's, followed by a stop along the river were intense, but Paul's shaving challenge and his mystery guest proved to be too much.

There was just one place to shelter before this inevitable meeting.

It was an original building, in fact, the only building on the property when Paul first purchased this land. The previous owners were a family with a dream to own land, something that would not happen if they stayed in Italy. The government's advertisements abroad promised large amounts of land for those seeking adventure, but, perhaps more importantly, more space to call their own.

What many didn't realize was their life could not be duplicated in this new place; in the case of this family, they did build a small shelter and broke enough land to begin farming, but were unable to grow enough food or secure enough winter clothing to survive. In fact, just two years into their three-year commitment, the only surviving member of the family wished to sell the property and return to what she knew in Italy.

Paul offered a more than fair deal and soon her neighbors wanted to sell as well. Acquiring large amounts of land became more of Paul's focus than fulfilling his responsibilities as the assigned Indian and Immigration Agent. He picked up the tools and learned the trade of barbering and continued to offer legal advice to those in need. In his other spare time, he built his home and, when I came to live with him, made the homesteader's shelter my private space.

As simple as it was, it was like a cocoon.

Although I never prepared the fireplace, Paul took it upon himself to chop wood and kindling so it was always ready to be ignited when needed. Once the fire started, I welcomed the heat radiating throughout; I didn't realize just how cold I was.

Stripping down to nothing but my well-worn flannel union suit, I wrapped a large wool blanket around me.

Just as I thought about the prospect of sleep, something I usually considered a luxury, I heard footsteps and his familiar voice. Paul always talked as he approached, a simple code between the two of us, but his was not the only voice I heard.

"Hannie?" Paul asked.

He wanted me to know he was there, but also that he wasn't going away.

"This is your private space. We both respect that, so we'll sit right outside the door," Paul said.

"Sorry to bother you, Hannah," came a man's voice, one I didn't recognize. "I'm here with news of your father," he said, emotion softening his voice. "He died a few days ago."

There was only one person who would feel this emotion for my father; a person who, as a young boy, aspired to wear the red coat of the now reconfigured North West Mounted Police. A boy who wished his father was Thomas Wright.

Samuel Peters.

Before giving my actions a second thought, I opened the door with the blanket wrapped around me.

My grandfather gave me a nod and left the two of us alone.

Although he was much older than when we last looked at each other, I was temporarily transported back to my childhood. Sam, only a few years older than me, and I spent hours dramatizing imaginary outdoor games.

Our friendship was similar to the one I shared with Night Star; the difference was secrecy. Sam and I could be friends for all to see, whereas with Night Star, it was a sacred friendship no one knew about.

There was only one challenge to my friendship with Sam. His mother, Beth.

She tried, on many occasions, to forbid Sam from being my friend. When Sam asked why, she simply told him he was too old to have a friend so young. Somehow, we still found ways to cross paths; sometimes at school, most times when I came to town with my father.

Sam had matured, now taller with a bit of silver showing at his temples. My mind scattered, remembering him as a friend, and now noticing how much more handsome he had become. With my mind muddled, I waited for him to speak first.

"You really do look a sight, Hannah," he smiled, slipping his hands into his trouser pockets, a trademark habit his mother abhorred, but, apparently, hadn't been successful in eradicating.

"So do you," I stepped aside and welcomed the only person I trusted other than my grandfather into my private shelter.

I sat on the floor beside the fire, offering up the only available seat, what I called an ancient wicker rocking chair, to Sam.

I couldn't help but think back to the very last time we played together. Really, we were too old to be playing the games of our childhood. Somehow, we'd escaped and found ourselves in a triangular open field shaped by the boundaries of my father's property, the proposed reserve land and Sam's grandparent's property.

This open space was now a battlefield. We were always on the same side, our trusty weapons, tree branches.

Sometimes the battle was based on a recent history lesson; sometimes we created a futuristic battle; but on this day, we were characters from an imaginary land, a land likely inspired by pirates, or at least what we assumed pirate-like warriors sounded like.

The battle was short-lived, as we'd just begun to try out our new pirate-infused language, shouting words like "blazes" and "bootlickers" and "bastards", when something distracted us both simultaneously.

Turning towards the distraction revealed the worst of our fears. It was Sam's mother.

Beth was always tense, not just when parenting her only child, about everything.

Anytime she walked into a room, I felt obliged to do something useful, as it was clear idle play was never acceptable behavior in her world. My newly braided hairstyle seemed only to make matters worse.

When she sharply called Sam's name, I felt awash with shame. Shame for the way we were playing, for the language we were using, for being where we knew we were not supposed to be.

Turning away, Sam simply followed. That was the last time we saw each other.

"How is your mother?" I asked, thinking it to be the most honest way to connect my memory to the Sam beside me.

"She's still the same, maybe a bit more uptight. Still never pleased with anything." He shook his head, smiling. "We should have run away that day."

I couldn't help but laugh. "And survive on imagination alone!"

"Might have been easier," he said, glancing cautiously my way.

There was such honest gentleness in both his manner and his words. Despite knowing Sam was here for other reasons than reminiscing, I surprised myself by remaining calm and still.

"He died a long, slow death," Sam said, trying to hold his voice steady, but I heard his sorrow.

I waited respectfully for a few moments before sharing my sarcastic condolences. "You are entitled to grieve his death. In my mind, he died when he sent me away."

Sam started to respond, but paused before continuing. "New information was discovered shortly after you left, sensitive information requiring confidentiality to ensure the investigation brought justice. His refusal to die had as much to do with wanting your forgiveness as it had to do with—"

He interrupted himself to see if he still had my attention and my permission to continue.

"Colonel Wright wanted you to see how much he'd changed." Sam reached into his coat pocket to retrieve a photograph. "He asked me to show you this," he said, handing me a photo with the image facing downwards. "He wondered if not for him, maybe you would come home for them."

I made no effort to look at the image.

Sam stood before making his offer, "I'm taking the morning coach home. If you consider what you've learned and want to see for yourself, I have paid fare for you."

He respectfully closed the door behind him.

I waited long past the sound of Sam walking then riding away.

I offered myself comfort with my usual reminders: there was no need for me to leave, no need for me to look at the photo. In fact, the fire blazed in front of me, tempting me to turn the photo into ash as I had done with all other things related to Colonel Thomas Wright.

Instead, I moved closer to the light of the fire to better see the image.

Three pairs of eyes stared back at me.

I recognized the face of my father, but not his eyes; gone was the steel-cold glare of discipline. Present was a softer expression of—I didn't know. What did I see? Compassion? Illness? Something else?

I did not recognize the face of a young girl, but there was something familiar about her eyes: dark in color, kind and curious. It took me a moment to remember: her eyes were the same as Night Star's.

The third was the face of a woman I'd never met. No one would question that she was the mother of this young girl, thus, Night Star's mother. I think I heard myself gasp as I drew my investigative conclusions from the past and this photograph.

I couldn't help but look again, this time at the trio.

While I understood the image captured them looking at the photographer, they appeared to be looking at me. Although each person was unique and separate, they were connected to each other.

They were a family.

My father's new family.

Before I could analyze further, Paul slipped quietly into my cocoon. He added a bit more wood to the fire before settling, as he always did, on the chair he loved so well.

"How long did you know?" I asked with what little energy I had left.

Paul took the photo from me. "Thomas told me himself. Just before you came back. His death and this photograph change things."

He handed the photo back. "The only reason Sam showed it to me was to ensure I didn't send him away. I told you, when you're ready to go home, you will make the decision."

I couldn't help but stare at my father's image. This was the man who at face value accepted the witness statements of outlaws rather than ask his own daughter for her truth. A man who assumed I was raped and thought it best to simply have me cleaned up and then sent to my grandfather's. A man who finally decided it was time for us reunite, and wrote me monthly letters, none of which I opened.

How could such a man have a change of heart of such magnitude?

Sensing my struggle, Paul lightly touched my shoulder. "I have long believed in the importance of finishing unfinished business. It's still your business to finish. When you are ready."

Standing, he added one more piece of wood to the fire, then left me with a decision to make.

Too tired for anything but what I needed, I curled onto my right side, knees tucked to my chin and drifted into a restless sleep knowing the nightmares were sure to visit.

WHEN OUR FEET *finally left the water, settling into the muddy shore, I wished I was not a girl; I was being looked upon as I had seen men look at prize livestock.*

One of them whistled, "Real nice night for a romantic swim."

Again, that menacing laugh. "By the light of the moon."

The silent one aimed his gun in the direction of Night Star's horse, and just before pulling the trigger, lifted upwards enough to startle but not harm the horse. Being a creature of flight, she bolted.

"Looks like you've been a bad, little Indian boy." He spoke to Night Star, but taunted us both.

I no longer cared which one spoke. Night Star gave my hand a strong, long squeeze. I squeezed back.

"Get your hands off her." A gunshot grazed his foot beside mine after the command.

Night Star released my hand and stepped forward.

*As if insulted by his approach, two men rushed
forwards, using their boots and the end of their guns to
force Night Star from his feet to his knees.*

*This brave act of submission deflected their attention
from me; by silently receiving their blows, his strength
mocked theirs. Winded, both paused.*

Night Star lay unconscious on the ground.

*A third man pulled me away and roughly put his hand
over my mouth.*

*Being only aware of what was happening to Night
Star, it took me a few moments to realize I was on the
ground, my cries stifled and my body pinned beneath
his.*

On My Terms

I BOLTED UPRIGHT. SWEATING.

Recalibrating my location. Grateful it was a dream yet disappointed to be alive and remembering.

Lowering my head to my knees, I waited for my nausea to abate and my heart rate to regulate, and wondered if my nightmare became more real with time or if my memory matched the horrors of my experience.

Damn that photograph, the mysteries of my father's new family begged to be discovered.

I lifted the floorboard and extracted a saddlebag, packed and ready to go. Not that I planned to go home; I planned to be ready to leave whenever I needed to.

But I would not make this journey by coach.

If any part of Sam's boyhood-self remained, he would welcome my invitation to skip the wagon and ride the trails.

The best time to be in front of Turner Creek's only hotel was at dawn. It remained a mystery how a such eloquent building and sophisticated concept could exist in this wild part of the world.

The Turner Hotel was newly built in anticipation of the expansion of the railroad and the lumber industry—this was not designed for the laborers of these industries; it was intended to attract business owners and their wealthy investors.

Guests had not yet risen. The tavern's doors would remain closed until after breakfast was served and any patrons in need of sobering up were out of sight.

I also knew the coach back to McLeod was scheduled to depart at six o'clock. As I recalled, Sam was seldom on time, thus my calculations suggested he'd be, at best, rushing but running late.

Sure enough, through the drawn sheers of the front foyer, I watched him juggle one bag as he rushed to the desk to clear his account, while simultaneously working a comb through his hair.

Turning, he near ran towards the door, clearing the steps two at a time. He raced past me without even a sideways glance. I waited. His peripherals delayed. Then he stopped in his tracks.

Pivoting, he smiled at the sight I presented to him.

"Looks like my favorite way to travel!" he said, reaching into his pocket for a few remaining crumbs. "As they know, you can judge a man by what he has in his pockets!"

Jack enjoyed human contact with only a few chosen few. Apparently, Sam was one of them.

"We'll go together, but I won't stay for long," I said, offering up the reins of an athletic mare in desperate need of a long ride.

"Promise you'll stay for two things?" he asked, warm and welcoming, yet indicating a desire for me to commit. "The first, obviously, meet the new members of your family. The second, is the reading of the will."

I nodded, thinking this should be a two-day commitment.

"And something else," he said, focusing on attaching his bag to the saddle.

I watched him guardedly.

"McLeod is very much as it was. Which is the primary reason your father wanted to see you before he died…you are essential to the continued prosperity of his family," Sam finished, now sitting astride.

"How are they prospering?" I couldn't leave that comment hanging.

"You are about to find out." He grinned and motioned for me to lead the way.

We turned the horses down the road just as the coach pulled up in front of the Turner Hotel.

"Are you still always late?" I teased.

"I'm always right on time," he shrugged and eased his horse in line behind Jack.

If we followed the road south, we would arrive in McLeod a couple of hours ahead of the coach.

I was in no hurry to get there so I guided Jack off the road and headed slightly west.

"Have you ever noticed how humans create paths of least resistance?" I asked pointing to the road we just left. "But animals create paths that ensure the most nourishment." I finished my question by motioning to the trail in front of Jack. At first glance, the clusters of shrubs were densely blocking any sort of a trail.

"Looks like we're taking the path of nourishment," Sam said, up for an adventure. "You are certain this will take us where we need to go?"

"Would I ever lead you astray?" I said, feigning innocence and enjoying a bit of my own humor.

As we approached, the dense cluster of shrubs revealed the trail I was seeking: soft underfoot with the right amount of moisture remaining in the sandy soil.

This wildlife trail to McLeod did meander a bit, but I monitored the location of the sun to ensure we would arrive by nightfall.

While we did stop periodically to offer the horses an occasional sip of water from the Spitzee River, by midday it was time to give them a full rest.

As if planned, the trail opened to a meadow caressed by the river on one side, framed by the mountains on the other and outlined perfectly by a cluster of aspens.

Once under the shade of the trees, I slid from Jack's back and promptly loosened the saddle bags. With the heaviest of his cargo removed, I pulled my saddle blanket from his sweating body. Relieved of his burden, his withers quivered in the luxury of this welcome reprieve. Finally, I lifted the halter from his head, thus completely transforming him into his greatest natural self.

To thank me, Jack gently rubbed his forehead against my shoulder before making his way to the stream. Only then did I stop to wonder where Sam was.

As I turned, I saw Sam's horse similarly stripped of its excess baggage. The mare joined Jack at the water's edge. Although she wasn't completely certain of her newly formed opinions of Jack, she didn't seem to mind sharing this refreshing moment with him.

"As usual, the animals are tended to first," Sam grinned as he lowered himself against the shaded tree. "Care to?" He playfully lifted a dusty boot in my direction.

"When you have four legs, no hands and carry this," I said, pointing to the pile of saddlery, "I might consider taking your boots from your feet," I teased.

"That smile—" he hesitated, then changed his mind. "It's been a long time."

Unsure of the proper response, I nodded as the smile evaporated. "It'll be cooler in a few hours."

"You'll get no complaints from me." Sam's voice sounded drowsy. With that, he slid further down the tree, folded his hands across his chest and closed his eyes.

I watched him in utter disbelief. Surely, he must be kidding. Seconds later, his breathing changed from soft breaths to deep, near snoring inhalations. As sleep seldom visited me for long periods of time, I was in awe watching sleep arrive so quickly and so deeply and so effortlessly.

My definition of resting had little to do with relaxing. Sitting with idle hands made me feel useless. Without my usual chores for distraction, I searched for something to keep my hands busy and my mind from wandering.

Only my boots seemed in need of attention. Slipping them from my feet, I was amazed by how fresh air proved to be such a welcome yet simple relief. Using a clean cloth from my pack, I wiped the dust from the leathered surface.

"Rested eyes are more useful than clean boots." Sam's voice, though low and gentle, startled me.

"That's it, five minutes?" I asked.

"Just enough to give me the energy to stay awake and atop that plodding mare," he smiled, pulling himself upright to a seated position. I realized he could probably say anything to anyone and get away with it if he smiled afterward.

"Walking is always an option." I finished one boot and started on the other.

"Observations and complaints are two completely different things. Tell me some of yours." He paused.

"Complaints?" I asked.

"Observations. How have I changed since I last saw you?" he asked and grinned again, knowing full well there were numerous and obvious differences since the last time we were together.

"You're a lot shorter than I remember. Less hair on the head, more on the face." I watched the smile fade as he tried to determine if my words were in jest. "And you've lost your sense of fashion." I nodded to the dusty, but obviously new, uniform.

"That's it?" He sat up.

Feeling sorry for his wounded ego, I eased up, "But your smile is still charming. Just as I remember it."

His recovery was immediate. "My turn."

"To clean my boots?" I was in no frame of mind to be analyzed by anyone, not even a friend like Sam.

"You are definitely taller. But are you taller than me?" He stood upon finishing his question. Taking my hands in his, he pulled me to my feet, turned us both so our backs were touching and then traced an imaginary line from the top of his head to mine. "You are finished growing?"

"If I have my grandmother's genes. But, if I take after my grandfather—" My pause was deliberate as I found myself reveling in his fear of being shorter than me.

"The hair is the same color. Is it still wavy?"

The temperature of my face intensified. I felt flattered by the attention, yet unnerved with his directness. My response was a mere nod.

Knowing full well my discomfort, he gently touched the tops of my shoulders, calming my apprehension with his smile. "I'm glad you decided to come back."

I watched him resume his reclined position under the tree.

"I don't plan on staying long," I said, pulling my boots back on my feet.

His nod was silently in agreement, but his eyes spoke the opposite. Holding a gaze without words, he suggested my scheduled departure may be a challenge: leaving McLeod might not be as easy as I envisioned.

Home

G LANCING AT THE sun now reaching its highest point in the day, I knew we would arrive in McLeod much earlier than I had hoped.

"You seem know these trails very well—why haven't you gone all the way to town?" Sam asked, riding beside me now that the wildlife trail veered towards the mountains, forcing our transition back to the road. "How many times have you ridden this far, then turned back?"

His tone was a challenge, so I countered with sarcasm. "I only rode to the best part. There is nothing beyond here worth looking at."

"You never had the urge to see him, just one last time?" Sam asked, genuinely curious.

"I didn't choose to go away." My tone was curt; the conversation, however short, was becoming tiresome.

"But you chose to stay away," Sam pressed.

"Now, my turn," I changed the subject.

Sam pretended to fear my question.

"Why did you follow in his footsteps? Or rather, how many of his footsteps did you follow?"

"The one thing we shared when we were younger was a desire to leave McLeod," Sam said, looking ahead, knowing the town would present itself soon. "But I wanted to do exactly what your father did. I wanted to attend the Royal Military College—"

"In Kingston," I finished for him.

"My timing was perfect given the need for more military and police to ease illegal trading and—" he cleared his throat before elaborating.

"I am very aware of the many laws being broken." I gave him the space he wanted. "Don't you think it funny, us being such good friends growing up in McLeod and then being so close when we both went away to study?"

This is a vast country so it was a significant observation to make, one Sam would completely understand.

He nodded. "Funnier still that we both had an interest in the law."

"The difference is Paul wanted me to study the law. You wanted to enforce the law and be like the man you respected," I added.

"And yet, it seemed like we were worlds apart," Sam said.

"Does Beth approve?" I shivered saying her name out loud, but I had to ask given how protective she was of Sam.

"She sees nothing positive in anything. I always hoped she'd soften with time, but her bitterness increases each year that passes her by." Sam shrugged.

We rode towards the town in silence, giving me time to take in all that came into my view. When I left, Fort McLeod had just been rebuilt in the town rather than on an island between the Spitzee and Alberta Rivers. Back then, there was no promise of a north and south railway, let alone one that would be constructed from the east to the west. Thus, the fort had only the essentials: police barracks and military surgeon's office, a small mercantile trading storefront and a blacksmith.

Sam stopped at a newly situated graveyard beside a small but stately Catholic church. "A bit bigger than you remember?" he asked.

That was an understatement.

While we were on the edge of the town borders, the fort was nowhere to be seen.

Instead, a well-groomed road invited travelers down a street lined with impressive modern homes, some with fences, others with gardens.

"It does look much more sophisticated than it actually is," Sam said with a bit of cynicism.

I let Sam take the lead. Jack wrestled with my instructions; being a follower was not of his liking. Pressing my legs firmly to his sides while holding the reins close, he finally acquiesced.

As we plodded onward, I silently cursed the faint light ending the day. Jack felt my emotions, his body ready for a sudden command to take flight.

Just when I thought control would no longer be mine, Sam's smile coaxed me to his side.

"We've covered miles of dust, melting snow, mud and heat, yet you find this to be the most difficult." Sam decided silence was not a good approach.

Maybe logic would help, so he continued, "Think of it this way. You agreed to meet your family and hear of your father's wishes for you. After that, your future is your own. No one will keep you here against your will. When you need to leave, you can leave."

He reached over to place a comforting hand upon my own. "And, I'll be close by to help if you need it."

He was right. I'd come of my own volition and I could leave on those same terms.

"I just need to check in at the barracks—the coach arrived several hours ago and I was supposed to be on it," he said, lifting his eyebrows with light-hearted suspense.

"I'm sure there's a surprise party planned?" I said, my tone getting edgier.

He laughed, "Believe me, there's nothing I'd like better than to celebrate your return. Instead, allow me to give you the grandest of tours." Sam made a dramatic gesture as if to unveil a marvel. "May I present the town of McLeod at dusk."

Keeping a slow pace, Sam rode reassuringly at my side.

"Some things never change." Sam nodded to his left. "Though I'm sure many of the younger folk wish it would!"

He stopped in front of Clarkson School.

"With so much growth, yet the school remains the same." I shuddered at the memories of school.

While I loved learning, I struggled with the confines of discipline and sitting still.

"Same place, same schedule, even the same headmistress until last week!" Sam announced.

I couldn't believe Miss Johnson remained the school headmistress after all these years.

Sam continued onwards towards the barracks, and while I could see the shape of that familiar building before me, I admit to feeling agog when noting the number of businesses lining the street beside me: The McLeod Gazette, Mountain Majestic Hotel, Madelaine's Books and Millie's Millinery.

Time changes many things, but such significant changes for what I considered to be such an insignificant geographic location? I shook my head, reconciling the discrepancy.

The new McLeod barracks were impressive, much larger than the original fort, reflecting the ongoing theme that McLeod was a town on the cusp of major growth. Surely the railway alone was not the sole reason?

"It's a large, empty space most of the time," Sam said, the look on my face must have conveyed something other than curiosity. "I'm sure you'd love to say a quick hello to my mother?"

I was certain the question was in jest. "She wasn't on my must-see list."

As Sam secured his reins on the vacant post, the office door opened. Light from within outlined Beth's figure. She was never an attractive or a handsome woman, but the finery of her wardrobe served as a camouflage.

Tonight, she wore somber shades of greys and blacks. Beth stepped stiffly down the stairs and, head held high, walked towards us.

"Samuel," she said, her voice demanding an explanation rather than offering a greeting.

"Hope my change of plans didn't worry you." Sam bent to kiss her cheek.

There was no affection offered in return.

"Hannah's returned for the reading of the will," he explained, moving aside, no longer protecting me from her piercing stare.

"Better late than never, I suppose. Welcome home, Hannah," Beth said, her tone sandwiched reluctantly between terseness and politeness.

Before I could reply, Sam handed me a piece of paper and glanced across the street. "Can you go ahead? Just give one of the Clarksons this and I'll be there before he's done?"

Relieved to be released from further scrutiny, I nodded, finding it humorous be back in the role of running errands.

Sam gently tucked his hand under Beth's elbow and escorted her down the wooden sidewalk, leading her away from the barracks. Beth couldn't resist casting one last glance in my direction.

Holding my ground, I waited until they were both out of view.

Across the street, I saw a familiar sign on a much larger than I remembered storefront. Clarkson's General Store stood proudly on its foundation, tempting any and all to step inside to have a look.

Given the enlarged frontage, I was not surprised to see the shelves were stocked, loaded with more than necessary. To simplify the layout, one side could be categorized as needs and the other as wants. I was so taken by the contents, I paid no attention to who was inside.

"Wonders never cease," a voice crackled, part man, part boy. Neither tone rang any bells of familiarity.

"A wonder indeed," an Irish accent added playfully.

I turned to face two men; one, I assumed to be the youngest of the Clarkson family and the other, a man likely four or five years older than Sam or I, yet his eyes glinted with more youthful mischief than we could muster.

"Welcome home, Hannah." The young Clarkson wiped his hand on his apron and extended it in earnest welcome.

Before he could get another word in, the Irish gent stepped elegantly between us.

He too extended a hand, but not to shake. Bending at the waist, he lifted my hand towards his mouth. "A warm welcome to you, young Hannah from afar."

Once his lips respectfully touched the top of my hand, he stood up and took his hat off. "Master Barnes. New to the community. New to the country for that matter, but not new to the profession that brought me here."

Not wanting to be outshone by Barnes, the young Clarkson stepped between us. "James Clarkson, the youngest in the family, but surely the most intelligent!" His voice crackled more as he struggled to sound like an adult. "We were sorry to hear of the passing of your father."

Not wanting to continue the conversation about my father, I nodded to James and then spoke above the top of his head, "How is it you passed the scrutiny of Beth?"

"After such a brief introduction, how is it you so easily guessed my profession?" Barnes tried to look affronted.

"You have the appearance of one who teaches, but your attire suggests you are accustomed to a wage much higher than that of a headmaster," I summarized my appraisal with a lighthearted tone.

"Is there any chance you seek continued education?" Barnes smiled warmly.

"I finished with that learning—"

"Beth did say six o'clock," James interjected.

I had to give it to this young Clarkson, he was sharp and he was competitively jockeying for my attention.

"Indeed. To keep such a woman waiting would be a mistake. I do hope I have the pleasure of your company in the not so distant future?" Barnes said, bowing gracefully and then leaving.

I was surprised to find myself amused by his charm and his harmless flirtation. Most of my experiences with such interactions left me feeling in need of a bath. Although I didn't indicate otherwise, I, too, hoped our paths would soon cross.

"My mama says no woman in McLeod will be spared," James said, sounding very much a teenager, laughing nervously. "You probably don't remember me, but my brother, Randy, had some serious crush on you when he was younger."

Before I could ask more, the front door opened, signaling the arrival of new customers. James knew his job, attending to business, but I was distracted by intense voices coming from the back of the store.

Following this conversation, I slipped through the swinging doors separating the merchandise for sale from the merchandise for inventory.

Two men faced each other, one with hands on his hips, the other with eyes cast downward, holding a beautiful leather pad saddle.

While I was intrigued to understand why this transaction occurred at the back of the store in a secluded entrance, I could not keep my eyes off the saddle.

It appeared supple as a blanket, yet the leather suggested it offered a structure that would ensure comfort for both the rider and the horse. Beyond that, the embroidery and the bead work were exquisite—so elaborate, perhaps, it might be more suited to be sold as a valued, framed work of art as opposed to one designed for a horse and rider.

The man with the saddle was an age somewhere between my grandfather and my father. The other, who I assumed to be Randy, kept an unnatural distance between himself and the saddle.

"How could I possibly sell something so poorly constructed," Randy spoke loudly with unnatural pauses between his words. When he reluctantly touched sections of the saddle, he did so as if it was covered with burrs.

Even from this distance, I speculated it was likely worth three times what was being offered.

Clenching my fists, I watched Randy standing as I had seen so many men stand, intimidating another by position or race. My inner loathing would either choke or churn; I was in no mood to passively stand by. Just as I decided to intervene, a familiar hand clamped firmly on the top of my shoulder.

Sam read my eyes, but his common sense overrode my impulsive intentions. Placing another hand on my other shoulder, he turned me around, and ushered us along the outer edges of the store and out the front door unnoticed. I took deep breath. Again. My heart pounded inside my rib cage and vibrated in my ears. My limbs tingled.

Sam led me to Jack and assisted me onto my saddle. Though Jack snorted disapproval, he accepted the reins being tied to Sam's horse. Sam was in charge and I settled in, knowing the next stop was out of town.

The town refused to accept me before. I doubted it would this time, regardless of the contents of my father's will.

McLeod was the last place I wanted to be, but here I was. Temporarily.

Introductions

RETURNING TO A childhood home should stir up memories, yet, as we moved along the trail, I felt no such nostalgia, or I had buried the memories so deep they no longer existed.

There were two well-worn lanes etched in the ground, indicating this was a path much travelled. Approaching the main entrance, there was a sign marking property, not with my family's last name but with a title: The Preservation.

The house beyond bore no resemblance to the house I left behind.

Gone was the Victorian style two-story home, much like those I'd seen while studying in Toronto, only ours was made with logs not bricks.

In its place, a one-story modest log home.

While the previous structure seldom welcomed me—I frequently schemed ways to be outside rather than inside—

this one presented like open arms, begging me to come closer and step inside.

Before Sam could offer any explanation, the front door opened.

Stepping from the warmth inside appeared two silhouettes: a woman and a child. Judging by their tentative steps and guarded stances, our hearts beat with the same uncertainty.

It was the child who shifted first. She smiled.

I looked towards the woman. She smiled.

Both Sam and I dismounted on opposite sides, connecting in front of our horses. Sam wrapped a protective arm around me and guided me closer. "Hannah, I'd like you to meet Ivy and Bryn."

The memories I was waiting for sprang forth in the form of sorrow. My mind tried to rationalize the impossibility of these two having any likeness to Night Star. Yet, in a smaller more feminine way, they did. I wasn't haunted by the similarity; I was saddened by the stark reminder that Night Star no longer lived. I drove my fingernails into my palms to sharpen my focus.

Just when I thought I had stability, a small hand pulled my right fingernails from my palm and nested itself into mine.

"I've been waiting to meet you my whole life," Bryn gushed, looking up at me with utter admiration.

Lowering himself to one knee, Sam took Bryn's other hand in his. "I told you she'd come to meet you one day. Well, today is the day."

"We are honored to have you." Ivy offered a hand in welcome as Bryn reluctantly released hers from mine. "He told us you would return. We are grateful. I'd like to honor your father's wishes by letting you sort though his affairs in the solitude you deserve, but first, we ask that you share a meal with us?"

It was a sincere invitation from Ivy, but it was an expectation of Bryn's.

Sam stood up. "Go ahead. I'll be back in the morning. Promise you'll stay at least until then?"

Because I didn't trust myself to speak, I nodded.

Relieved, Sam pulled my forehead to his lips. The touch reassured me that he would support and protect me if I let him. In this moment, I needed his support and protection and, surprisingly, his affection.

Bryn interrupted our silent connection by tugging on my shirt, encouraging me to follow her into the house my father built for his new family.

Aside from the completely different architecture, what I found most curious was the openness of the home. At the center was a massive double-sided stone fireplace, unlike any I had ever seen, with a cast-iron cooking stove on top. The table was set for three guests. Whatever was cooking smelled delicious enough to shift me from feeling unsettled to feeling hungry.

Bryn guided me to one chair and promptly settled onto the one next to me. Ivy stoked the fire before ladling a caramel-colored thick stew into three separate bowls. With the bowls in each of our places, she took the seat across from me.

"Salud," Ivy said in Spanish. She lifted her spoonful of stew towards me and then to Bryn. "We welcome you home, Hannah."

"Your home is most welcoming." I politely returned the gesture by raising my spoon.

We ate in comfortable silence, giving me time to take in the rest of the house. There were no walls separating the sleeping from the eating, the eating from the sitting; two doors were the only indicators of separation and both opened to what I assumed to be the outdoors.

"This new home was designed by your father after spending months with the First People in what we call our longhomes," Ivy offered.

Not many can read my thoughts, but I knew I was gawking, "I have seen similar concepts, one open area, with the homesteader shelters built by early settlers but I have never seen one constructed so elegantly with wood."

"One of the many riches on The Preservation are the trees, so much so, the government tried to renegotiate the land titles to ensure they'd have an abundance of timbers to build the railway south and north. While we fought that offer and saved the trees from excessive deforestation, we selected only what we needed for this house." Ivy paused looking upwards. "We had much help with the construction, but the design was all your father's."

"He even planned your house," Bryn announced. "So you could live with us but in your own house."

It was a statement.

No, it was a fact.

Bryn expected me to live here.

Seeing my discomfort, Ivy added, "It really is a smaller version of this house, one we lived in while this was being built. It serves as a guest house." She smiled. "While we love to do everything in the open, not all our guests wish for the same."

"And…we have a surprise." Bryn looked to Ivy for approval. "Is it time, Madre?"

Ivy shook her head, entertained by Bryn's lack of patience. "I think so. Would you like to tell Hannah your surprise?"

"We made you a welcome—" Bryn interrupted her own thoughts as she leapt from her seat and reached under the drapery covering the cupboard contents. Delicately, she lifted a small round cake out and up, announcing, "A special apple cake for you!"

Bryn wasn't interested in discussing the cake, she was on a mission to share it.

Before even finishing the last of my stew, my bowl was replaced with a small plate featuring a perfectly sliced piece of apple cake. Bryn stood beside me, hands clasped behind her back. She was irresistible.

"It's been a great many years since I've eaten—"

"It was your mother's recipe." Bryn, finishing what she thought was my sentence, was thrilled with their gesture.

"Bryn, let's give Hannah a moment?" Ivy looked at me, smiling as she shook her head. "We have been trying to work on listening as well as contributing to the conversation. As you can see, Bryn has a lot to say."

Bryn, wanting to show me her skill, stood silently.

"I don't remember my mom's cake, but I bet this tastes as good or better than hers." I took a bite and nodded in appreciation.

Bryn proceeded to slice the cake and share it with Ivy before devouring hers.

"It has been a long day and I feel, for you and for Thomas, it is time for you to read his final words to you." Ivy's voice faltered. "Bryn, please wish Hannah good night?"

Bryn slid off her chair and wrapped her arms around my shoulders, resting the top of her head against my neck. "I love you, Hannah. Thank you for coming home."

Had I ever felt such a rush of genuine, innocent affection?

My hand touched hers as I whispered, "Thank you for welcoming to your home."

Ivy, ever aware of the need to proceed, stood and motioned us toward the door opposite the one I entered. It was at this moment I noticed two details I had somehow missed. The first was how petite she was; in the family photograph, my father was seated, giving her the appearance of being near his same height. The second was her coloring; in the photograph and when I saw her in the doorway, I saw her as my mind assumed her race to be: I assumed she was born to one of the nations, perhaps Blackfoot. But now, I saw her coloring to be more from a Spanish background, making me curious about what path led her from wherever her home was to being Night Star's mother, then Bryn's mother and now my father's second wife.

As we walked along a narrow, wooden path connecting their home to the guest house, I refocused on my surroundings. I could see a silhouette of the roof line against the night sky. As Ivy described, it was a miniature version of the family home.

Entering the guesthouse, I saw completely the opposite. It wasn't a guest house; it was an office with a cot serving as a guest bed.

"This was Thomas's office. It is also where he chose to spend his final days," Ivy said, standing at the door.

It was as if he was still there. Many of the items on top of the desk looked as though he'd been working, but just stepped away from his desk for a moment.

"You must wonder why Bryn calls Thomas her father," Ivy said, her back to me as she lit the prepared cast-iron stove. "Her skin color is that of her birth father, Morning Owl. My first husband and Night Star's father."

Turning to me, her eyes held me accountable to be honest with her.

"I did wonder. Her skin is as beautiful as Night Star's was," I replied, barely a whisper.

"Your father loved her as his own, once he reset his path. He adopted her to ensure a layer of the law might ease her future struggles," Ivy said, her hand lovingly caressing the top of the desk. "This box is yours. Thomas wished that you read his final words as soon as you arrived. But I thought it best to share a meal. This room, our home and this land are ours: mine, yours and Bryn's. You will need to hear many more details, but for now, stay and reconnect with the man your father had become."

She moved to the door. "You know where to find us if you need anything."

And there I was.

Alone. In the room where my father took his last breath. All I needed to do was sit in that worn leather chair.

Did I need to know?

More to the point, did I even care to know?

It wasn't the death of my father that compelled me to open that box; it was Ivy, Night Star's mother, that did.

I opened the box.

A letter, neatly scrolled and wrapped with a magenta ribbon sprang upwards almost enthusiastically.

He had written countless letters to me, none of which I opened, leaving him no choice but to write me one last letter, a letter he hoped I would receive and read.

There was no mistaking the handwriting. While other aspects of his life had so obviously changed, the dignity of his penmanship remained truly his and his alone. No man or woman could imitate his articulate letters. His style was as good as his signature.

I held the letter to my heart.

For a moment, I was reminded that our relationship had not always been strained.

My Dearest Hannah,

Death has invited me to visit for more than a year now.

Each day I refuse the invitation to leave the land of those I love so deeply.

Each day I ask for just one more day.

Each day I'm granted, I hope to see you for, much as I love Ivy and Bryn, it is my unfinished business with you that keeps me alive.

If you are reading this letter, I have no days remaining. I've waited too long.

If I were a better man, I would have asked more questions and not sent you away on that day. I was limited by my blindness, blindness to the realities of a cruel world I was unknowingly part of orchestrating. Thus, I have this last opportunity to tell you how I came to be the man you wished your father to be; the man I was before your mother died.

Once we had gathered nearly the last of the Blackfoot Confederation and signed Treaty 7, granting them land and financial support, I rode through Fort McLeod.

What greeted me were not the faces of a once proud, vibrant nation, but hungry and fatigued souls with no option but to surrender their way of life and their spirits. They trusted us to find a solution, but we had created a new, much worse problem.

It was then I realized a small nation called the First People had refused to sign.

White Feather and his son's widow, Ivy, asked for my time. They were considering moving westward, seeking an alternative to signing Treaty 7. Instead, they proposed receiving land, the very land they had lived on long before settlers, police and other nations, but no financial support.

The land they requested was, at the time, not considered desirable.

They also shared, in perfect spoken English, the loss of Ivy's son, Night Star, the boy whose murder you witnessed. There is more to this tragedy, but I've asked Sam to share those details when he feels the time is right.

This conversation put me at a crossroads: continue with what I had been assigned to do or resign from my post and create something different.

You are integral to the survival of The Preservation. My words in a letter cannot possibly reveal all there is to know. Simply, my possessions and my land are now in your name, as you will read in my last will and testament.

As Ivy will explain, doing so is the only way to ensure Bryn will have every opportunity she wishes to pursue. I know you are pursuing yours, and Ivy hers, but Bryn is still young and thus extra protection must be put in place for her future.

When you've gathered all the information, Ivy and I expect you to do what you need to do. I have no right to ask any more of you.

Over time, maybe you will be able to forgive me?

Aside from sending you away at a time when you needed me the most, I regret never telling you how much I loved you. I'm telling you that now. Allow me this chance for you to start over, not with me, but with those I left behind.

I rest in peace knowing no one will ever send you away again. You have my eternal love.

Your father,

Thomas Wright

I lowered my head to rest on the top of his desk.

Ivy was right; it had been a long day, but this letter made time itself feel like an eternity.

Long days I could deal with, but facing a long night trying to avoid sleep, knowing nightmares were certain to resurface?

Maybe if I found someplace outside I could stay awake but rest. I lifted a wool blanket from the bed and slipped out the door.

The breeze against my face reminded me of my freedom. As I walked away from the light and the security of my father's office, the bottoms of my feet felt the familiar ground beneath me. Sure, the fence, outbuildings and house were different, but the land was that of my childhood.

All I needed to do was find that one place where I could think and eventually rest.

Before opening my eyes, I knew where I was, but given it was dark when I arrived, I had no idea how I got here. Lying on my side, the wool blanket under and over me, I noticed the setting of the moon marked the start of a new day.

When I elected to sit, a foot pressed me back to the ground, the force was not to comfort, but to threaten and dominate.

"The coward returns," an unfamiliar voice growled.

The foot released, allowing me to move, but I knew it best to stay on the ground.

"Get up." The commanding tone left me only one option.

Before me was a young man, likely not from the town of McLeod, but perhaps from the reservation I assumed to be nearby. He was furious, so much so, I wondered if my night adventure resulted in me crossing the property lines.

I needed to test the situation. "Only cowards attack those asleep."

It was a feeble attempt at sounding confident.

"I waited while you slept; now I can attack with honor," he said, standing too close for comfort.

My first error was to stand and relax, thinking this was my opportunity to use words to learn more.

Nonchalantly, I brushed the dirt and grass from my blanket.

He grabbed both of my shoulders and pushed me backward until my back slammed against a fence post. For a moment, I lost my focus, stunned by the force of his anger and the sharp pain along my entire spine. The last thing I wanted was to lose consciousness. By the time I stabilized, there was no question who had control.

His black eyes pierced my own.

Never had I been so scrutinized with hatred of this magnitude. In the event I was uncertain how he felt about me, he spat in my face.

"I'd like to ensure your stay is brief. You will leave this place, dead or alive. I will decide. Not like Night Star. You gave him no choice but death," he said, transferring a hand from my shoulder to my neck. "Perhaps I could recreate such a moment for you," he said, applying more pressure.

Had he a knife, my throat would have been split.

Had he a gun, my brains would have stained the very post I was pressed upon.

Had he not heard footsteps, he might have settled on simply strangling me on the spot.

As it was, he chose to leave. Vanished as soundlessly as he probably arrived. Though free to move, I remained pasted to the post.

"Hannah?" Sam took a couple of long strides in my direction. "What are—" Sam halted, looking beside and around me for any sign of threats.

I must have looked like I'd seen a ghost, but seeing no danger after assessing my condition, he pulled me to him. Of all the things for me to think about, I only focused on the freshness of his shirt, almost savoring this moment of being shielded protectively as opposed to finding ways to protect myself.

"Did you think I broke my promise?" I asked, pulling away from his embrace.

He smiled, relieved to find me. "When I checked the guest house, I was certain you left until I noticed Jack prancing like he'd lived on the ranch his entire life."

Looking around once more, he continued, "I went with my first intuition; you always did head for the hills."

For the first time in the light of this new day, I looked around. Hills did indeed surround us. No wind. No sound.

"I've been home less than twenty-four hours, and the first question I want to ask is, who hates me the most?" I asked.

He frowned. "Tell me what happened."

"So far this morning, I've had my body bashed against a fence post, been spat upon, and instructed to leave, dead or alive, preferably dead," I summarized.

"Sun Eagle found you already?" Sam shook his head. "Ivy told him you would be returning, but we didn't think he would do anything."

"Should I recognize this name?" I asked, a bit stunned this aggressor was so easily identified.

"Night Star's spirit brother. At birth, their parents vowed one to be the spirit protector of the other," Sam explained.

"And so he blames me for Night Star's death," I concluded. I now knew why he loathed my very being. "Any others I should be aware of?" I asked warily.

"That depends on how long you stay," he teased. "Sun Eagle is never far from Ivy and Bryn. He's taken it upon himself to protect them from threats...although Ivy has more protection than she'll ever need. I wouldn't worry, he's more bark than bite. Come, Ivy makes the best oat cakes with honey."

Sam slid his arm around my back, walking at my side and casting a protective glance behind.

Stay or Go

THE DOOR SWUNG open before my boots touched the top of the stairs. Bryn stood anxiously in the doorway.

"I told Madre you wouldn't leave without saying good-bye!" she victoriously announced, folding her arms across her chest with a proud grin.

"I didn't say she left, I said she wasn't in the guest house," Ivy said, shaking her head. "Somedays I wish children were still seen but not heard!"

With amazing ease, Bryn stepped beside me and slid her hand in mine. It was both novel and a comfort to hold a hand so warm and so small.

"Speaking of not being seen, weren't you just about to do something? Something important?" Ivy pointed to the south pasture.

Before Bryn could negotiate, Sam intervened, "Bet if I help, we'll be back in time for fresh oat cakes?"

"And honey?" Bryn added, eager to leave with Sam, but also anxious to return quickly.

"And eggs," Sam added.

"Breakfast will be on the table by the time you finish." Ivy pretended to shoo them away.

Bryn might have been mesmerized by Sam's offer, but I knew his actions to be deliberate; he wanted to give Ivy and I time alone.

In a way, I was grateful.

We could work together with a common task of preparing breakfast and I could tell her my intentions. I followed her into the kitchen.

Kitchens have always been my favorite room in any house. Even though my mother died before I had lasting images of her working in the kitchen, I always had a nanny and they all loved to cook.

Ivy poured me a cup of coffee. Judging by the color and texture, this pot had been simmering for some time. Perhaps she slept less than I did.

"I was hoping to leave by the end of today." I didn't want either of us to settle into a degree of comfort with each other's company.

"Would you stay if Bryn and I left?" Ivy asked after taking slow sip.

Her genuine question reflected pure selflessness compared to my selfishness. This was not my home, yet she was offering to leave on my account.

"He was your father; this is now your ranch," Ivy said, sitting comfortably across the table from me. It was as if we'd known each other before meeting yesterday, and this conversation, however challenging, was simply the one we would have.

"He was your husband and Bryn's father. More of a father to her than he ever was to me." The coffee somehow made my bitter words flow and the pauses feel more natural.

"Whether we wish it or not, we are tied to your decision. If you stay, we can stay. If you go, we must go," Ivy spoke matter-of-factly. She appeared to be more than prepared for either outcome.

"My leaving should have little or no impact on you and Bryn," I said, wishing it to be true, but wanting to hear more as to why it wasn't.

"You and I can dance politely around this, but the reality is we have very little time. The land, that now belongs to you, borders that of the First People. It yields prosperity. It is perfectly located for easy trade between the borders, but the people who live and trade in McLeod rejected me as a person when I married my first husband." Ivy paused. "I'm not certain which they despise more: the people they call Indians or the white woman who married an Indian chief."

So, she wasn't born into one of the nations.

My original prediction was nearly confirmed given my presumption Ivy and Bryn were fluent in the Spanish language as well.

Ivy was right. Word of my father's death would create much more interest in the acquisition of his property, thus threatening the stability of the First People's property.

I knew the undercurrent of racism ran wide and deep; Ivy would have a difficult time trading first and foremost because she was a woman. Add to this the fact she also had a history with the First People, or rather had become one of them, which further complicated her position.

"Between the hired help, when I could get it, myself and members of the First People, we have prospered when so many around us have not. With his passing, my name carries no authority. It may seem as if I'm pressuring you to stay. But I'm not. Bryn and I have had a wonderful life here, but another, equally wonderful life awaits on the other side of the property."

"My reputation in McLeod may have even less authority than yours," I said, fishing to see how much of my past she knew.

"Your father told me there was but one person who could overcome the narrow minds of this town—he often spoke of his daughter, the firebrand! He thought your personality was genetically aligned with your mother and your grandfather. He described your strength as being greater than the barriers that would be placed before us. And, if my son was a true friend of yours, I have no doubt as to your strengths."

This double shot of respect, both from the land of the dead, was powerful, reminding me just how appealing kicking up the dust might be for us all.

"I can't say how long I'll stay." Now I was talking without thinking.

"I'll ask that you stay until your soul directs you to leave." Ivy lifted her mug to seal our deal. "Salud."

Before we could discuss the business further, Bryn burst into the door and plopped herself on the chair. Sam followed a few moments later.

"I've never fed chickens in such a short time." He stopped, out of breath. "It looks like we were much more efficient than our kitchen staff!"

Ivy and Sam stepped aside to start the food preparation while Bryn rested her head on her arms neatly folded on the table, and stared at me.

Allies & Enemies

I SUSPECTED THERE WERE many details Ivy and I should discuss, but the priority was to send me back to McLeod with a long list of supplies.

Standing outside Clarkson's store, I studied the list. It was obvious Ivy been waiting some time to restock her barns and her kitchen. I wondered when my father's illness changed his ability to go to town.

Given what I'd witnessed the day before, I could well imagine how she would be treated if she came here on her own, especially now that she was his widow.

Today I was in no mood to barter with manners. This order would be filled with a better than usual price.

I opened the door to begin the process.

Fully expecting to see a gathering like Earl's, I halted at the awaiting vacancy. It was a temporary luxury to think I would have the store to myself until I heard hushed tones from somewhere in the store.

I knew where they were coming from, but I wanted a surprise entrance. I stepped back out the front door and made my way along a narrow dirt footpath to the back of the store.

It was Randy and the same elder as yesterday.

This time it wasn't saddlery he attempted to trade; it was a small stack of sheep skins.

"These have not cured properly," Randy said. To add emphasis, speaking louder and slower than necessary, he picked one up and gave it a shake.

I was no expert, but this was a beautifully prepared pelt that would be worth a lot of money given the raw fleece had been picked, cleaned and combed, ready to be used as a rug or comfort covering for furniture.

"My offer or take this out of my sight." Randy's tone was intimidating.

I knew exactly what he was doing.

"How much for all four?" I asked, stepping forwards then running my hand over the pelt with the fleece intact.

It was divine.

I wasn't sure of this elder's understanding of English or his comfort with my being there, but I knew he would understand the currency of the bills I pulled from my wallet.

Randy looked at me, smiling only for me to see.

"You know as well as I do these are worthless." Randy continued his condescending tone while trying to engage privately with me.

I had to admit, I was stunned—Randy thought I was on his side, bartering for an even more competitive price alongside him.

"What did you offer?" I asked, curiosity getting the better of me. I wanted to know just how low he would go.

The currency was snapped out of my hand before a response was offered. Turning towards the money, I realized I was staring once again at Sun Eagle who was probably eavesdropping on the conversation longer than I was. He looked no more pleased to see me than he did when I woke to his miserable face earlier this morning.

"My father will have nothing to do with your money," he said.

For emphasis, he tossed the money at my feet, then gathered the pile of skins in one arm and extended a hand to his father. Without a sideways glance, they were gone, leaving Randy standing awkwardly beside me.

"That was a good, quick lesson on how to deal with those people," Randy said, his confidence restored, extending a hand to shake mine. "They have no business sense, squandering opportunities presented to them, and live in poverty when property grows like the weeds around their shacks," he added, shaking his head in disgust before changing expressions all together.

Realizing I was not responding to his hand, he continued.

"Welcome home, Hannah," he spoke as if I was joining his team.

"Those people thought they had a good business deal when they signed the treaty agreement," I said.

Randy took a step back, eyebrows lifting in disbelief.

"I thought I might find you here." Sam's timing was not appreciated, at least not by me.

Randy was obviously relieved with the interruption.

Sam took the list from my hand and handed it to Randy. "We'll come back to pick it up later today?"

Randy skimmed the list and enthusiastically nodded.

I would leave this. For the time being.

Sam dismissed us by tipping his hat, placing his hand under my elbow and escorting us through the store and out the front doors.

Once we were a safe distance away, he paused, "You can't change decades of patterns by being a tornado. If you have agreed to stay, for however long, you now need to think about Ivy and Bryn." He took a breath as if to cultivate more patience. "This is a time and a place where you must think before you speak." He spoke as if to coach rather than belittle my passion.

"Who did you think I was thinking about back there?" I said.

Despite his efforts, I didn't like his tone; probably because he was right. I had been too focused on my anger, not on their wellbeing, which was why I was at the store in the first place!

"You were just being you, but remember," Sam said, taking another patient pause that was fast becoming too familiar, "this is about bridging your father's business so Ivy and Bryn, and maybe you, continue to prosper."

"I don't want to make this worse. But I also don't want to accept what is," I said, feeling my temper simmering down.

"It's a perfect time to understand what is," Sam motioned to the storefront behind him. "Then you can explore what it might become?"

The way he said it made me wonder if he was talking about the ranch or something else. It was then I realized I was distracted by Sam's appearance; he was dressed for duty, making him look even more impressive. Did I really want to think about my childhood friend this way?

He was a man and, given my promise to myself, I would have very few men in my life. Those that were would be family, friend or business acquaintances.

Sarcasm seemed the best deflection.

"Seeing as you know so very much, I trust you'll teach me how to deal with the rest of the finer citizens of McLeod," I said, sounding childish, but that didn't stop me from folding my arms across my chest.

"With pleasure." Sam took a bow and tipped his hat.

"Samuel," Beth's voice eerily interrupted.

We froze, both recognizing the voice, then turned toward her, acting like a couple of ten-year olds caught doing something we shouldn't be doing—which, in Beth's mind, we were.

"I was quite certain your duty today was on the northern outskirts," Beth said, staring down her nose at my clothing, still the same items I had on the last time she saw me. She was dressed for the day and it was another work of art; a symphony of royal blue satin all in different layers and textures from her hat all the way to her shoes.

"Perhaps you'd like to have a bit of a chat with your wayward son in private, madam." Barnes appeared beside her, winking so only I could see.

"Thank you, kind sir. I would indeed," Beth said and angled her elbow, commanding Samuel's hand.

Sam turned to me before they walked away. "I'll bring the order back later today," he said, sheepishly shrugging his shoulders so Barnes and I could see.

"Tis a great pleasure to meet with you again." Barnes stepped into the space where Sam just stood. "And, while Madame Peter's tour of this town has been enlightening, I've a feeling your version may be a bit more entertaining," Barnes said, his voice and accent sounding like a song.

He started walking and I, almost in a trance, followed.

"Walk with me a while my wild, western beauty." Barnes invited me in such a way no one would refuse.

His charm was fresh and irresistible, but mostly it was a welcome distraction.

"Hmmm, where do I begin?" I narrated with an exaggerated intonation. "This town prospered first on fur trading, then whiskey trading, followed by backroom property trading until truly settling with a rail line connection south and north. Now, for a select few, there's money to be made from ranching, lumber and, in the very near future, coal," I summarized without any trace of admiration or respect.

Barnes looked ahead, his face intently taking in my brief description.

"Let's start with the whiskey trading…I've a mind to explore a similar business for myself in the future," Barnes said.

"Whatever you do after teaching, remember, this land first belonged to others. Now they have very little and yet this town seems to prosper," I said.

"You see the reservation people differently," Barnes said, genuinely interested.

"I see them as people. I know them as people," I said, simplifying my perspective.

"But I understand you have been away for some time. Are your opinions still valid?" he asked, gentle and respectful.

"I'm sure Beth gave you her own colorful version of me. But I assure you, it was more than likely inaccurate," I replied, feeling a tinge of anger that Beth, given all she would need to tell Barnes before assuming his duties of the new headmaster, felt the need to share gossip about me.

"Stories are one thing; I prefer to form my own opinions. Perhaps the town has changed?" he offered, cautiously optimistic.

I wanted to paint the true picture of McLeod. Conveniently, we stood in front of the saloon; the window sign was all I needed.

Pointing, I said, "I prove my point."

A massive sign hung above the double glass doors: White Men Only.

"Sadly, 'tis similar signage in some places in my home country. Things that are said in a pub are often not fit for women's ears," he said, now playing the diplomat.

"Why don't I find out for myself," I said, feeling more reckless than diplomatic.

Barnes's eyebrows lifted. "You'd step inside, despite the sign telling you otherwise?"

"Care to join me?" I asked, standing in front of the double glass doors.

"I wouldn't miss this for anything," he said, smiling as he held the door open for me.

I put on an all-knowing face, but truthfully, I'd never been inside a saloon. Earl's beverage bar didn't count; he served sodas, not alcohol.

It was a slow day, only four men and two women were seated at a table by the window playing a game of cards. Talking ceased as we walked toward the bar.

Barnes carried an air of sophistication, maybe even money. I highly doubted these patrons would assume he was the new headmaster of the school.

Stepping into his role, he took the lead. "Two shots, kind sir," Barnes ordered, pulling currency from inside his coat pocket.

"The rules are clear. Men only," the man behind the bar said flatly and continued with his task of taking inventory. "If she needs help reading it, I'd be happy to oblige," he added without making eye contact with either Barnes or I.

Snickering from the card table.

"My money's as good as his, my thirst more appreciable," I said, pulling my own currency from my trouser pocket.

"If reading isn't your problem and I've explained the rules, I'll have no problem grabbing you by the scruff of your pretty neck and tossing you out as I've done with a great many others who break the rules of this establishment," the bartender said, now looking directly at me for some sign he could proceed with his threat.

"There are women allowed," I said, looking over at the card table.

Each one of the women was completely entranced by the brewing dialogue.

"Are you applying?" he asked, his tone degrading me from an illiterate to a prostitute.

"Not to worry, I know of a finer establishment with a more sophisticated set of rules," Barnes interrupted the escalating conflict, wanting to avoid where this lesson was heading; he extended a hand.

"Thank you, Master Barnes." Sam strolled in as if on cue. "Hannah's presence is needed elsewhere," he said, his eyes locked on mine, challenging me to remember our previous conversation.

I looped my arm through Sam's and Barnes's and we walked to the door. I heard every one of the lewd comments, but I was too frustrated to be embarrassed.

"I bid you both good day," Barnes said once we were outside the saloon. He tipped his hat and, in his usual fashion, bowed gracefully. "Thank you for giving me your version of this town's history."

Once he was out of earshot, Sam spoke sternly, "Two tornado stops in one day."

As we approached our horses, Jack pawed the ground, letting me know he was more than ready to get moving.

"I will bring the supplies this evening as promised. You and I will take a walk. No more stops for today," Sam said.

I knew he was frustrated, more likely simmering on a slow boil. Without uttering a word, I stepped onto the saddle blanket and cantered out of town as if I didn't have a care in the world.

Majestic

N O ONE WAS in the house when I arrived, giving me an opportunity to study the design in more detail. Whether I looked up, to the side or down, I felt like I was wrapped in layer upon layer of wood. Any fabric accents were designed, I suspect, by someone on the other side of the property fence or much further south like Ivy's childhood home; I admired the original designs, beautifully dyed and intricately sewn coverings made from wool, fur or hide. While I had lived in the comfort of my grandfather's home and the luxury of my uncle's home in Toronto, the level of artistry surrounding me made Ivy and Bryn's home seem more exotic than eloquent.

As peaceful as this home was, I felt the lingering agitation from my interactions in McLeod. There was one cure for my restlessness.

Stepping into the afternoon sunshine lifted my spirits. Knowing Jack to be busy impressing the mares, I decided to follow the fence in the opposite direction as my meeting post with Sun Eagle.

Though still hundreds of feet away, I spotted the purest example of magnificence.

Funny how, whether beast or human, the most beautiful creatures have a stance which, despite their unique markings, sets them apart from all others.

When I was within fifty feet, I knew this to be a stallion, one very much aware of my approach but remaining confidently aloof.

I leaned against the fence to take in the sight of him. He was of meticulous breeding—demonstrating the best markers of purebred Morgan lineage: notably, his upright graceful neck perfectly proportioned to his muscular shoulders and quarters. To make him even more stunning, his coloring was not the usual bay, black or chestnut. He was palomino, glistening with strength and smoldering with the potential of speed.

Curiosity can only be stifled for so long. When he lifted his head to finally acknowledge my presence, he looked instead to a space somewhere beyond where I was standing.

I knew horses to be creatures of flight, but he was staying. I followed the direction of his gaze to watch Bryn skipping along the path towards us.

To my amazement, this magnificent creature who had so elegantly ignored me, transformed into a frisky colt. His hooves literally danced in place before prancing towards Bryn, now walking along the fence towards me. When he reached her, he turned and followed her alongside the fence. It was as if she had him attached to an invisible tether.

As they came closer, Bryn looked upwards, opposite the horse and finished her conversation, "I will, Papa."

She ran towards me and slid her hand in mine.

"You found him," Bryn said, standing proudly but dwarfed beside the stallion.

"Is this beauty yours?" I asked.

"He was Papa Tom's," Bryn said, reaching under the top post, offering the horse the pleasure of her touch.

Of course, my father always rode the most spirited horses.

"Does he have a name?" I asked.

"This is Han," Bryn proudly introduced us.

Han's ears perked up and his body readied for whatever she might ask of him. Instead of ask, she reached into her pocket for several thoughtfully prepared leftover oat cakes. She giggled as his soft muzzle gently nibbled the treats from her hand.

Looking concerned, she turned her attention to me. "Don't tell Madre? She doesn't think horses should eat honey. But Han absolutely loves it!"

"I wouldn't dream of revealing your secret," I whispered. "Do you miss him…your papa?" I asked, curious to learn more about her imaginary conversation.

"He is always with me, but it's not the same as before," Bryn said, acknowledging the conversation I witnessed to be as natural as the sun rising and setting. She continued to focus on sharing her leftover breakfast with Han before turning to me. "Do you miss him?"

That would be a difficult question to answer with one as bright as Bryn, so I deflected with another question, "Why did you call him Papa Tom?"

Bryn shrugged. "It was kind of an agreement. He wanted me to call him something different than you did. Different from what I would call Papa Morning Owl."

Well, I stepped right into that one. Hearing her speak about the man I called my father in such a loving way was touching.

"You called him father, but you left. He didn't want me to leave, so I called him something else," she said, shrugging like this was the most logical solution.

So much pain.

So much silence.

So much misunderstanding.

And yet, Bryn settled into a space of contentment by accepting her reality.

"Who rides him now?" I redirected the conversation again.

"Madre says I'm too small. But I know size doesn't matter. Han's and my hearts are connected. He would never hurt me, and he knows I would never hurt him," Bryn said.

Han snorted in agreement.

"So this magnificent fellow is neglected," I said. "Where do you keep his tack?"

"Papa Tom never rode with a saddle. He told me if a rider needs a saddle to ride Han, Han doesn't need the rider," Bryn's voice imitated what I vaguely remember as my father's lecturing tone.

"I have an idea you might enjoy." I smiled at Bryn as Han finally decided to give me a closer examination by sniffing my hair. If I was a friend of Bryn's, I was a friend of Han's.

I agreed with her, Han would never allow her to fall.

I was only guessing, more like hoping, Ivy would not return from wherever she was for a while. It was a simple plan: use a light halter with a tether and lead Bryn to the house atop Han. I had a sense, if Ivy saw how naturally Bryn and Han connected, she would allow the relationship to grow as they aged together.

As we approached, Han walked gracefully, making it easy for Bryn to sit on his back without sliding off. We stayed inside the fenced paddock and walked the line of fence leading toward the house.

Ivy and her horse approached from the road opposite to our path. I watched her, deep in thought, slide wearily from her saddle only to sense she was not alone.

When she looked our way, I knew Bryn was grinning from ear to ear.

Ivy stopped.

We stopped.

"I told you I could do this, but see, we were careful," Bryn said with an air of childish confidence.

"You were ready a long time ago." Ivy's eyes misted. "But I wasn't."

Ivy walked towards the fence and admired the partnership. The closer she got, the more regal Bryn and Han looked.

Ivy patted Han's side flank, distracted by her own thoughts. "Let's leave the horses and walk a bit? It's time to show you a bit more of The Preservation," she suggested.

While we could have ridden, it seemed a brilliant idea for the three of us to walk. It was a gloriously warm day.

After a short walk up a hill, we stopped and Ivy stepped aside. "Tell me what you think," she said, sweeping her hand across a low and wide valley.

I was not prepared for the sight before me.

Sam and Ivy called this a ranch, but until this moment, I had yet to see any livestock. I assumed they ranched open range cattle like so many of the new ranches in the area. In the fenced pasture below, the size of the herd was astonishing. But there was not a cow to be seen.

"So this is the ranch," I said.

Ivy nodded. "There have been so many cattle losses over the years. Disease, weather, theft. We decided to change from cows to sheep. And we have been most fortunate… the sheep are easier to manage and appear to adapt better to the ever-changing weather. There is also a unique market for cheese and wool, both of which we have yet to fully explore."

I knew the concept of ranching was expanding, both in the number of ranching families as well as different types of livestock being explored. This was the first sheep ranch I had seen. Ivy and my father had a different relationship and a different perspective. It made perfect sense they would create a different style of ranch.

"It was your father's idea. We are also developing another business: tack and saddles." Ivy turned away from the herd, resting one elbow on the fence before adding, "I find the sheep leather easier to work with and quicker to cure."

"I think I saw someone trying to sell one at Clarkson's," I recalled Randy's bartering from the other day.

"That was White Feather. He offered to see how he would be received." Ivy paused. "We will have a difficult time selling any of our products now that your father is gone…this is part of what you must consider if you stay. While the town has its own reasons for blocking my business, they may have different reasons for blocking your prosperity."

It was disconcerting to think such an innovative ranch would not be part of Bryn's childhood. If I was being honest, I was becoming more intrigued by The Preservation than anything I'd seen thus far.

"He said you would be there for us, but I didn't want to get my hopes up," Ivy said, looking at me. "I know your memories are not ones you wish to remember. But maybe we can create new memories. Together?"

The invitation was touching.

And truthful.

As if on cue, Bryn's hand slid into mine. I was growing increasingly comfortable with the strength Bryn transferred each time she demonstrated her affection for me.

Here we stood.

Three women with an innovative ranch on the cusp of flourishing in a place governed by men.

A Different Invitation

IVY WAS NEGOTIATING a transition for Bryn's bedtime, so I stepped outside on the porch. Dusk began wrapping the ranch in a soft blanket of indigo darkness.

I couldn't help but think the sheep ranching plus tack and saddlery business were brilliant. To make it all work was foundational on the continued alliance of the First People and Ivy. They had worked well to date, but my father was the axle, the one with strong business and legal connections.

Now that he was dead, my arrival would most certainly roughen the surface for future negotiations. In fact, as Ivy indicated, there was already interest by local prominent landowners to purchase the entire perimeter of The Preservation.

It was a lot to consider given I had my own reasons for wanting to leave.

To distract myself, I wondered if Sam would keep his promise to bring supplies and visit later.

No sooner had I wondered when the thunder of horse's hooves and wagon wheels echoed down the hill. Someone was indeed approaching with plenty of speed, but very little control.

By the time the wagon entered the yard, the horse slowed to a full stop. Odd, there was a horse and a wagon, but no driver. I walked warily toward the horse, now standing still and breathing heavily.

"Easy now, easy does it," I said, keeping my voice low and calm before extending my hand toward the harness to deter further movement.

"Easy does it, indeed!" Barnes's hatless head appeared from the rear of the wagon. "The beast is positively possessed!"

"It really is easier if you sit in the driver's seat. Horses are intelligent but not automatic." I laughed at the disheveled version of the Irish headmaster.

He was perspiring more than the horse.

"I was in that seat until we hit a rather large bump. Once I was dislodged, the beast took over, but somehow we arrived where I intended to go." Barnes sounded as exasperated as he was frightened.

Now regrouped, he stepped awkwardly from the wagon and took a customary bow.

"And what would brings you out here this time of day," I asked, truly curious.

"It's been a rather long evening meeting parents," Barnes said, regaining his usual demeanor before inquiring further. "Is it customary for so many women to spend so much time with the headmaster before classes resume?"

"I suspect you may be a bit of a novelty, being the first male headmaster," I said.

"I've been a good many things, never a novelty," he said, dusting off his trousers one more time, then placed his hat over his heart. "But I've another question to ask."

He shuffled his feet.

"You may not be aware, but there is a community gathering tomorrow evening, to celebrate the town becoming incorporated. And I was wondering if you might accompany me…in case I need an interpreter." He smiled.

"You'd ask me this after my behavior this afternoon," I teased back, having absolutely no intention of spending any more time with the community than was required.

"To tell the truth, I found your actions to be scandalous. And I enjoyed every moment," Barnes said.

"What would the town's mothers think if my actions were more scandalous tomorrow evening?" I asked, giving him every opportunity to change his plans.

"I've no fear. I am officially the headmaster and, given what you've disclosed, they are fortunate to have me." His chest lifted a little. "Besides, I'm paid for my expertise in academics, not romantics."

He was flirting in such an entertaining manner I found myself warmed by the conversation. It felt foreign, yet so comfortable to be with this man I had only recently met.

My response escaped before I had time to dissect and analyze, "I'd be honored to be at your side." I pointed to the wagon. "On the condition I meet you in town. If I'm going to do this, I want to arrive in one piece!"

"A sensible plan," he looked at his horse and shook his head, "for us both!"

I took Barnes by the elbow and, imitating his style, walked him towards the wagon.

"Would you mind me giving you a few tips before you travel back from where you came?"

"I'd be much relieved," he said as he climbed up.

I guided the horse around to face the road leading away from the house, and then handed Barnes the reins.

"Stay in the seat," I said and gave the horse a pat, confident Barnes would arrive safely home.

Ivy joined me on the porch, curious as to the visitor that left so quickly after arriving. "I was certain I heard you speaking with someone."

"That was the new headmaster, Master Barnes," I said.

"I wouldn't have recognized him," she said. "Like you, Bryn has been schooled at home."

I had nannies, well-educated nannies, who provided my education, making me curious as to who was teaching Bryn.

"Do you her teach in English or Spanish?" I asked, hoping this question would open the conversation for me to discover how this woman of such sophistication ended up in a place like McLeod.

As if reading my mind, Ivy offered an explanation, "I must seem a contradiction…I was not quite twenty years old when I travelled here from St. Louis. My father—I was well educated, with more ambition than I should have—didn't want me to waste my life in the pursuit of a business or a vocation of my own!"

Ivy shook her head, deciding to refocus. "Although my plan changed radically when we arrived, so did my father's I might add. It was that fine education that has served Bryn well. Attending McLeod School is not an option for her, but she will be very well-educated in the hope times will change so that she will have numerous other opportunities."

Ivy's silence meant two things: either the conversation was over or she had something significant to say. Her silence signaled the end of this conversation, opening a different space for my new, rather frivolous problem.

"Barnes has asked me to attend the town's gathering tomorrow," I announced, already regretting my acceptance. "What on earth will I wear to such a silly event?"

Clothing had never been a detail I had given much serious consideration. From the moment of my mother's death, my nanny and my father were concerned with cleanliness and practicality. After I befriended Night Star, and became more stubborn, I wore clothing suited to boys and then later, to men. While I wouldn't go so far as to give males credit with superior intelligence, they seemed superior when it came to prioritizing practicality regarding clothing.

My attire was simple: trousers and shirt, tailored for my frame, and boots. I suppose it seemed a trifle ironic that I, on the eve of this social event, found myself considering my fashion options. "What is an acceptable ensemble?" I asked.

"Your father used to attend many events every year. He never wanted to go, but he knew it was good for business. And it always was," Ivy said, a mischievous grin emerging. "Maybe you would like to wear something of his?"

"You can't wear boys' clothes." Bryn's voice startled both of us as we thought she was asleep.

She stepped onto the porch acting like we'd been sitting there waiting for her.

"Girls can wear boy's clothes and boys can wear girl's clothes. It's just clothing," I teased, keeping a serious look on my face.

Bryn considered my logic for a moment. "But you can't wear Papa Tom's clothes to a dance."

Wise beyond words, she was right. Besides, even if I wanted to, nothing of his would fit.

"But you could wear Madre's clothes," she offered. Confident she was on the right track, she disappeared back inside.

"I do have some things that would be suitable," Ivy offered.

"Why didn't you go with him?" I asked. "Or do I already know the answer?"

"It was about the business." She shook her head. "While I helped build our business, it was best if I stayed in the background. I suspect most assumed I was the hired help."

Ivy stood. "This hired help needs to help someone...fall asleep this time." Ivy smiled and stepped inside.

Once back in the guest house, I drifted into a deep, dreamless sleep, so deep I didn't hear Sam's horse or his arrival with the Clarkson delivery.

Arrangements

I SPENT MUCH OF the day at my father's desk. His business, since aligning the property of the First People with his own, was immaculate: dates, accounting, bank notes, contracts and transactions all recorded with impeccable detail.

I knew him to be accomplished in the police work he did when I was a child, but this illustrated something other than just running a business.

He was on a mission, a mission that just might make way for an unimaginably prosperous future. If investors thought the purchase of The Preservation would be easy, they were in for a shock.

I still had several ledgers to review when the door opened.

"You've stalled long enough," Bryn said and motioned for me to follow her.

What greeted me was a room transformed from a place to sit by the fire to a place to bathe—a large iron bathtub with wood trim and legs had been retrieved from some mystery location. From where I stood, I could see steam rising from atop the edges.

"Off with those dusty clothes," Bryn commanded, trying to sound like a sergeant. Then she giggled. "Come see what Madre added to your special bath!"

I didn't need any more coaxing. Stripped of my clothing, I slipped into the milky water. Ivy had indeed gone beyond just warm water, she added a bit of milk plus a few dried wild rose petals to add a hint of fragrance.

"Hair first, Bryn will do the honors," Ivy said and handed Bryn a small bottle while she released my braid. My scalp tingled as it always did when my hair was set free.

To speed up the process, I slid my head under the water and stayed immersed for a few moments before resurfacing to the smell of rosemary.

"Your father said you should have been born a fish, or at least somewhere closer to an ocean or a lake," Ivy's recalled, her voice calm.

"This is Madre's special shampoo, can you smell—" Bryn interrupted herself. "This is my favorite part," she continued, massaging my head and neck.

So as not to create more work by asking them to keep the water warm, I suppressed my longing to soak a bit longer.

Once the bath was complete, my hair brushed and drying, it was time to talk clothing.

"You need something less casual, but not too fancy," Bryn summarized what must have been an earlier discussion. "We've picked some things of your mother's and some of Madre's," she said, pointing to the space I assumed to be my father and Ivy's bed.

Draped over the edge of the bed were three possibilities.

The first was a rose-colored gown, somewhat faded into a unique color; it was simple in embellishments and beautiful in style. The second was emerald silk, fitted at the top, flowing at the bottom. The third was a white blouse with subtle lace around the collar and cuff, paired with a long leather skirt trimmed in beaded patterns of wild flowers along the hemline.

"We have each guessed which one you'll pick," Ivy said and glanced at Bryn. "But she knows which one she'd like you to wear."

Bryn sat at the edge of her seat, loving this entire process—clearly savoring a young girl's sense of fashion.

"Okay. I pick the blouse and skirt...and Bryn, I guess that you wanted me to wear the emerald gown," I asked, testing my prediction.

The look on her face was pure astonishment. "How did you know?"

Ivy and I laughed.

"Well, my selection was easy. This is as close to a girl wearing trousers as I can get. Green is a beautiful color for you, Bryn—that dress will look gorgeous on you in the future," I said, hoping it offered some consolation.

Bryn beamed and I thought: she will wear that dress one day and she will be beautiful.

"I do want to know about the one I selected," I said.

"It was my union outfit." Ivy's eyes misted. "To your father. A union is different than a wedding; a strategy we knew to be essential if I outlived him."

"Are you okay if I wear it?" I asked, feeling like I should reconsider my selection.

"I would be honored," she said.

It was long past time to get ready.

"Keep your eyes closed," Bryn instructed and held my hand, guiding me to the only mirror in the house. When we stopped, she maintained a strong hold of my hand before giving her permission. "Open."

I opened my eyes to see my reflection and promptly squeezed them tight.

"You don't like it?" Bryn asked, genuinely upset and concerned. "But you can only see your face!"

She took the small, round mirror off the wall and stepped back until she was satisfied I could see the reflection of myself from head to heel.

I opened my eyes again, honestly amazed.

At first, I doubted my own vision.

But on this second look, the transformation was unbelievably true.

The outfit outlined the curves of my body; not that I wasn't aware of those curves, just that I didn't know what they looked like on my frame outside of trousers and a shirt. My hair was lifted into a loose chignon with strands accentuating my face.

"I've never seen myself this way before," I said.

It was the truth.

"You are beautiful in your natural way and now, in this new look for business." Ivy wrapped a protective arm around my shoulder. "Should anyone refuse to talk business with you, we will all leave in the morning!"

It was in jest, but it was also the truth.

I didn't need to complete business tonight, I needed to pick up where my father left off.

"It's time." Bryn opened the door. Standing ready, dressed in a dazzling red and gold saddle blanket with matching halter, stood Han.

"Han took your father to such events; he'll gladly take you." Ivy supported me as I moved from the mirror to the door. "Maybe even more so now that his tack showcases his magnificence!"

I lowered to one knee before Bryn and asked, "Are you okay with me riding Han? He's your horse now."

"You and I can share him," Bryn beamed as she wrapped her arms around my neck, careful not to disturb my hair or outfit.

Stepping into the side stirrups and adjusting the skirt to align with my legs and the saddle, I sat atop Han. He was more ready to take me than I was to get there.

With a gentle touch of my heels, Han cantered up the hill, away from what was beginning to feel like my home.

Reintroductions

ONLY THE BLIND would have difficulty finding the location for this evening's event. At the center of McLeod, inner and outer lights gleaming, stood the community hall. If the lights were not enough, all one needed to do was follow the trail of parked carriages.

It was, in fact, the carriages that reminded me of my present reality. From what I could see, I was the only guest to arrive atop a horse rather than be pulled by one. I was travelling light, reflecting my intentions to not settle back into my childhood home. This was a temporary stop, like much of my McLeod business. This reminder put a little bounce in my step.

Admittedly, I was dressed for the part, but I needed to remember whose daughter I was.

While I had a reputation of being wild and unruly, and who knows what else after I was sent away, my father's reputation was quite the opposite—he was widely respected for his integrity and fairness.

Some of those girls who refused to play with me when I was younger, or taunted me with cruel words, would be here tonight, maybe even with young children of their own.

I felt my confidence weaken, wishing temporarily I was back at Ivy and Bryn's home.

I needed to remind myself yet again: they were the reason I needed to stay.

Barnes would be pleased to see me. That would be a start. After that, I'd make conversations with those open to talking with me.

As I secured Han, I felt a hand touch my elbow.

"He'll be fine out here waiting for you, but I wonder, will you be fine in there?" Sam's voice, always with a bit of humor, settled my resolve. "May I escort you to the door?" he asked.

When I turned to look up at him, he paused dramatically mid-step, pretending to be shocked by my attire.

"Perhaps I was mistaken? Who is this beautiful woman on my arm?" Sam teased.

"Take a good look. I'll be back to my usual in the morning," I said and resumed walking, now not certain which made me feel more uncomfortable: the event or Sam's appreciative glances.

As we neared the steps, I caught sight of Barnes peering anxiously into the darkness beyond the light. Judging by his face, he feared his date would not show.

When he noticed our approach, he assumed Sam had a date of his own, thus he continued to look away in anticipation of his.

We paused at the bottom step.

It didn't take long for Barnes to acknowledge who I was.

"My wild beauty, I thought you'd changed your mind," he said and skipped three steps, only to land on the ground in front of me. Assuming a regal manner, he gently lifted my hand and lightly kissed the top.

Sam, on the other hand, frowned. Maybe he was a bit annoyed with the discovery I had arrived to meet another.

"If you let me know when you delivered the order last night, I would have told you," I clarified for him. "Barnes invited me to be his date this evening."

Sam graciously transferred my elbow to Barnes's.

"Master Barnes, I believe your date has arrived," Sam said, his voice unusually neutral.

Proud to have me on his arm, Barnes led the way into the event.

"As the saloon refused to offer you a glass, I brought some of my own," Barnes said and discretely pulled a small flask from his coat pocket.

"You know the rules for alcohol are very strict. Men only. When they are at the saloon," I said, sincerely hoping his beverage would not be noticed by anyone but me.

"Rules are meant to be revised. This is a family tradition," he said and took a sip.

"Drink has never been one of my pursuits," I explained, even though we tried to order a drink yesterday to test the rules.

"Oh, I do hope to learn more of your pursuits," Barnes said and then tucked his flask away.

"You will need to stop by to see what my family traditions include," I said loud enough for Randy passing behind me to hear.

"Hannah," Randy said, nodding his head to acknowledge Barnes. "I wanted to ask you the other day—" Randy interrupted himself, taking a detour around yesterday's awkward encounter.

Regaining his composure, he asked, "Will you be selling the family assets now that your father has passed?"

I'll admit, Randy's forwardness was stunningly inappropriate.

I did us both a favor by saying nothing which, not surprisingly, Randy interpreted as permission to elaborate.

"I believe your father would have been proud to give my family first option to buy," Randy announced.

I honestly couldn't determine if he was daft or arrogant.

"If he saw the same kind of business I saw yesterday, I highly doubt it," I said, knowing just how sharp my words sounded.

Barnes, ever the diplomat, turned me to the dance floor. "Shall we leave business discussions for now?"

We left Randy standing dumbfounded and worked our way to the center of the floor.

"I have absolutely no idea how to dance," I said, standing seemingly as dumbfounded as Randy, but for completely different reasons.

"Then simply follow my lead," Barnes suggested.

Which I did, quite naturally, until someone tapped Barnes on the shoulder. That someone was in uniform, thus in a position of authority.

"May I?" Sam asked.

Without waiting for an answer, my hands were transferred from Barnes to Sam. "You are making a fool out of yourself." His words, however polite, scolded.

"A fool? For coming here and dancing like a few others from this community?" I said, glancing around to validate.

"He's flirting in an unacceptable manner. The man has kissed your hand more than a dozen times since arriving tonight. Who knows how many more before?" Sam's lead was firm, unyielding like his words.

To anyone watching, we were dancing, but I was genuinely confused. Sam and I were friends; this jealously was new territory.

"Samuel." Beth's voice shifted the tension between us.

Only one woman could cause Sam and I to freeze, guilty or not.

We turned to Beth and a lovely young woman I didn't recognize.

"Sam, have you made a proper introduction?" Beth asked Sam, but looked directly at me.

As always, despite my efforts to dress for the event, Beth's eyes scanned me from head to toe; the lower her gaze, the deeper her disapproval. Then her expression changed as she showered approval on the woman beside her.

Sam stood silently beside me, so Beth spoke in his stead. "Hannah, we'd like you to meet Anne."

Anne smiled sweetly, completely oblivious of the layers of messages being delivered and received. She stepped nervously towards me. "A pleasure to meet you."

She was lovely in appearance and innocent in her life experience. I assumed she had absolutely no idea who I was, but I knew Beth would enlighten her with her version before the end of the evening.

"This is Samuel's… fiancé," Beth said, enthusiastically emphasizing the word, as if their wedding was imminent. A smile formed on her face, something I had never before seen. It wasn't a smile of joy or pride. It was a victory smile.

"Excuse us for a moment. Master Barnes awaits your return," Sam said, guiding me in the opposite direction from Beth and Anne while avoiding Barnes.

He kept walking until we stepped out the doors and stopped on the very same set of steps he escorted me to at the beginning of the evening.

"Was there something you forgot to tell me." I couldn't believe what I felt and heard in my own voice. Jealousy.

"What Beth said is true. I am expected to be engaged. But not because I've officially proposed. It has been arranged for a year now. All I need to do is ask," Sam said, his voice flattened by his situation.

An arranged marriage seemed like something from a century ago. It sounded like an impossibility, especially for a man as honest and principled as Sam. But what should it matter to me? He was my friend. We'd been friends since we were children. The way I felt right now wasn't what a friend felt.

Business intentions vanished from my mind as I marched away from Sam towards Han.

Another Encounter

As I rode from the community lights towards the light of the half-moon, I instructed Han to walk. Strange. My escapes into the night usually involved speed and mindlessness.

Tonight, I needed time and I needed to think specifically about my changing feelings towards Sam.

I had always enjoyed his company, but something had changed. I noticed the way he looked at me was different, like he wanted to tell me one thing, but said something other than what I expected. His words were logical, but his expression hinted at a deeper, more mysterious message.

If I were to be truthful, I would have to admit I wanted to understand the mystery. I would have to admit I wondered about his intentions. Much as I might deny it, I had considered what it would be like if Sam was more than a friend.

But that would mean crossing into a whole new territory.

Paul had warned me about the coming of such an event. I told him the same thing I told myself: if I didn't allow myself to care for anyone, I wouldn't need to worry about someone becoming more than a friend.

Therefore, Sam must remain a friend, as I was not prepared to open that part of myself. Not after what happened to me the night before I was sent away.

Han halted, sensing something in the darkness. I could hear another horse heading towards us.

Before I could calibrate the direction, a horse and rider emerged suddenly from the darkness. I felt Han shift his location to avoid collision, but something smashed against my ribs, pushing me opposite to Han's movement.

I couldn't breathe.

I fell into a space somewhere between sky and land.

When I next opened my eyes, I was curled in a ball on my right side. While I hoped to find myself alone, I knew this not to be the case. A foot slid between the ground and my rib cage, nudging me the way one would to determine if something was alive or dead.

"Open your eyes." The voice sounded disappointed to discover I was alive. There was only one person who addressed me with such hatred. Well, Beth had a different way of expressing a different kind of hatred and, to be honest, I was more conditioned to deal with Beth.

"Sit up," Sun Eagle commanded with that all too familiar menacing growl.

Did I detect a bit of concern that I might not be able to sit up?

Not wanting to test my theory, I slowly transitioned upright only to feel a wave of nausea sweep over me. I leaned away from Sun Eagle and vomited. Finished, I scolded myself for missing his foot, a golden opportunity to express my feelings for him.

And then I drifted back to that space between land and sky.

"Hannah! Hannah, wake up!"

I heard a concerned voice begging for my attention. It was definitely Sam's voice but it sounded like he was underwater.

The more I tried to make sense of the voice, the more confused I felt.

I opened one eye, wondering how Sun Eagle could sound so much like Sam.

I felt two strong hands grip my shoulders, then lift me off my side and press me against his chest.

"Hannah." Sam's voice, usually calm, was taut with tension.

I curled into him, thinking it would be a relief to be so protected, but when I closed my eyes, I started to convulse with choking sobs. Sorrow buried so deep for so long seeped from me. I didn't recognize my voice or my body, but I surrendered to the sadness and to my vulnerability as I drifted once again to float between land and Sam.

When I next woke, I was still in Sam's arms.

Without leaving the comfort of his body, I asked, "How did you find me?"

"I followed you out of town after having a few words with Beth, but when I lost sight of you, I wasn't certain which direction you took," he said, gently pulling strands of hair behind my ears.

"Beth would love to introduce me to your fiancé now," I said, feeling a bit self-conscious with the remnants of mucus and vomit on my blouse.

"You are beautiful, no matter where or how I find you," Sam continued. "Han must have doubled back. What happened?"

"Either it was Sun Eagle or his near likeness who jousted me from my horse." I lightly touched the tenderness of my ribs. "So much for his bark being worse than his bite."

"Sun Eagle needs to be dealt with," he said and lifted my chin. "The story of that night and what happened to you has several versions, depending on who's telling the story. He seems intent on the version that makes you responsible for Night Star's death."

"Did my father speak to you?" I asked knowing, based on the letter I read, that Sam was one of the few my father trusted.

"He was led to believe, and there was a good amount of evidence to support, that you were raped by Night Star and then rescued by two traders who happened upon you both." Sam kept the summary short.

"Two?" I asked.

Sam nodded, not surprised by my question. "One of the men confided before his death, it was not Night Star, but a third trader they met along the way who raped you."

Sam kissed the top of my head and continued, "There was quite a collection of reports with ever-changing versions of the story, each one hiding more of the truth. Unless you decided to speak, we would never know what happened. But by then you were studying in Toronto. And he had other issues to deal with, namely, completing the treaty process."

Sam helped me to my feet although I still felt lightheaded and the pain along my ribs wasn't helping my overall stability.

Waiting until I could stand without his support, Sam added, "There are other details I will share with you when you're ready."

I didn't see any value in sharing the details of that night, his or mine. What purpose would it serve if Night Star had already been cleared of the accusation?

While I was here, I needed to do everything in my power to avoid Sun Eagle. Each time we collided, I paid a more significant price for witnessing Night Star's death.

Moving On

A MIRROR WASN'T NECESSARY. I knew I looked like I had been dragged behind a horse—well, not dragged, more like jousted off my horse.

Prairie Princess indeed.

Ivy and Bryn were in the kitchen, preparing breakfast to celebrate my first McLeod social event, although I'm certain they were expecting me to wake in my bed rather than arrive with Sam's support.

"Welcome—" one look at my appearance shifted Ivy into mother mode. "What on earth happened to you? Bryn go and feed the—"

"She can stay," I said, hoping my smile would put them both at ease.

Ivy somewhat relaxed. Her first thought upon seeing me was thinking the worst had happened. "Come sit."

Bryn just couldn't keep her eyes off me.

"Han is okay. I'm okay," I said.

Instant tears swelled as Bryn bolted from her chair and landed in my lap. I winced, but embraced her small body.

"We're all okay," I said, rocking this precious soul as I continued with Ivy. "What can I do about Sun Eagle?"

Ivy and Sam exchanged looks.

"I will talk to his father again." Ivy sounded frustrated.

"Before he can think of any more punishing surprise visits with me?" I suggested.

"No more punishments. What we need is peace. For all who choose to live here," Ivy said, pulling her chair closer to mine and caressing my arm. "Eat, then rest. We will talk business later today. Now Bryn, those chickens will not feed themselves!"

"Can you arrange for me to try selling that pad saddle at Clarkson's?" I asked Ivy.

"I can, but not until you rest," Ivy said, assuming the matter resolved.

"I'll sleep later," I said, knowing my tone was intense, but there was no way I would be able to sleep.

"Can I go?" Bryn asked, her head peering around the door, clearly eavesdropping as opposed to getting on with her chores.

Ivy and I couldn't help but laugh at her persistence.

"I'd love the company," I said and looked to Ivy for permission.

"The town isn't—" Ivy stopped herself.

"Nor is the land between here and the town," I said, reminding her subtly of my encounters with Sun Eagle well outside the town borders.

Sam scooped up Bryn as he entered the kitchen, enjoying a moment of playfulness, and offered some reassurance. "I'll meet them at Clarkson's. She'll be in good hands. Now, let's not let Hannah's breakfast go to waste."

Settling on the chair beside me, he finished what was left of my breakfast.

"Come and select what you'd like to sell." Ivy stood and I followed her out the door.

We walked into a small shop attached to the house, opposite to the location of the guest house. Ivy stood aside, letting me enter first. I stopped abruptly, certain my mouth was wide open in awe.

Ivy laughed, "It started as something I liked to do. But it has grown into a small industry."

On one side lay a stack of tanned hides, sheepskin to be exact; on another were spools of colored thread and bins filled with an assortment of beads; at the center, a large table carved in the shape of a horse with a pad saddle near completion.

"The pad saddle has long been used by many nations, but I've used the sheep hides to add more stability for riders not accustomed to being saddle-less." As Ivy explained, her hands caressed the beadwork. "I fell in love with nature when I first arrived. Every season inspires me to design new patterns."

The one she was working on was that of a vibrant mountain sunset.

"But surely you did not make all these yourself!" I knew her to be amazing in ways I had yet to discover.

"This may surprise you." Ivy looked at me to measure my response. "Your grandfather has been sending families our way for many years. Families who tried to settle in Turner

Creek, but found the climate, the weather or simply the people unwelcoming. We offered shelter and opportunity in exchange for their invaluable skills."

Ivy selected a larger pad saddle. "I will share more of that story when we visit the First People's village. For now, we need to consider something Han would agree to wearing?"

She pointed to an exquisite saddle, the leather darkened to charcoal with flax thread embroidery patterns of the sun and the moon in silver and gold.

It would look divine on Han.

Randy would find it irresistible.

Role Reversal

IT WAS A beautiful day for a ride, but before I could get Han ready for Bryn and I, Ivy stood comfortably beside me. I felt her struggle to be silent as she rocked side to side like the waves on an imaginary shore.

"You are surrounded by love, not only from this family you are getting acquainted with, but also from Sam," she said. "I know how much my son loved you."

We didn't trust each other to make eye contact.

Ivy continued, "You are in a challenging place, a place where you can change the future and reconcile with your past. I see the strength you carry within yourself…but I also see how silence closes your heart to freely give and receive love. It will do you good to spend time with Bryn. She is at that precious age when feeling love, seeing love and knowing love is as natural as breathing."

Silence was my way of dealing with my past, but it was also a convenient way to deal with what was happening right now.

So was having a job to do.

"We'll be back by supper at the latest," I ended the conversation.

There was business to attend to.

Bryn sat in front as Han walked with a graceful cadence, maybe even with a bit of pride.

While Bryn loved to talk, she was quiet for most of the journey. As we rode, I became aware that my intention to leave as soon as possible would not be as procedural as I anticipated.

Sure, I would be instrumental in finding a method whereby Ivy and Bryn could continue to build the business. That would not interfere with my leaving.

What would interfere was the dull ache I felt when I thought about leaving the two of them. And Sam.

This was to be a monumental change for me.

I'd been sent away. I'd run away.

And now I would find a way to leave, hoping I would see them again.

Once Han was secure in front of Clarkson's Store, Bryn followed me cautiously up the steps.

"Go ahead, I'm right behind you." I offered for her to take the lead, but she stood her ground. I realized she likely had never been inside Clarkson's.

I took her hand, stood beside her, opened the door and motioned for her to enter.

Once inside, she stopped again. This time, mouth slightly agape, staring up, down, over and across.

I had to admit, I'd been in stores of many styles and descriptions, but the Clarkson family had created something of a marvel. It might have been the mere quantity of goods throughout the store, but it was also how everything seemed to be displayed in just the right place to capture your attention.

For a young girl, especially one not accustomed to being in such a place, it was astonishing.

"Excuse me. That is not the door you are to—" Randy stopped moving and talking the moment he noticed me standing behind Bryn.

"Do you have a different door for royalty and important dignitaries?" I asked, my words sounding friendly, but my message anything but.

"Oh, Hannah. I didn't see you," Randy said, regaining his composure.

"While Bryn has a look around, kindly step outside with me," I invited, holding the door for him to exit.

Bryn stood frozen in place, her eyes wide with excitement and uncertainty.

"Go ahead. If you see anything delicious, we'll buy it." I smiled and followed Randy outside.

"Have a look and let me know if you have need for such in your store." I approached Han wearing Ivy's pad saddle, the very same design White Feather had attempted to trade the precious day.

"It is exquisite." Randy stepped closer, but hesitated given how Han's posturing threatened his safety.

Once I calmed the palomino by holding his halter, Randy took a closer look, touching the fine workmanship and attention to detail.

"I am in short supply of harnesses and saddles, but the demand is high. Especially with the more affluent wanting to showcase their wealth," Randy said.

"We don't have a problem with supply," I said, knowing he assumed he was seeing this product for the first time.

"I had no idea your father was running this sort of business. This would be a great opportunity for us to work together," Randy said, his confidence now inflated with what he perceived to be business acumen. He was near salivating with the prospect of selling this product and working with me.

"You do realize this is the very pad saddle you declined yesterday? The one the elder tried to trade?" I refreshed his memory.

Not believing what I said to be true, he took another look. "That is not possible."

"That is reality," I said and stepped towards the front door. "His hands are the ones giving us this opportunity to work together."

"I will need to speak with my father." Randy hesitated, another reminder of his lack of power with the family business.

"You have until tomorrow. If you are willing to make this deal, we'll arrange a time for you to come to The Preservation to see the other products," I said, opening the door for him, but politely blocking his entrance. "You know very well how connected my grandfather is in Calgary," I said, sounding factual while inciting competition.

I let Randy pass only to see Bryn waiting for us right where we left her. Her expression told me what I needed to know—I followed her to the counter to purchase what she had selected.

"I'd like to make one more stop," I said, lifting Bryn onto Han.

"You can make as many stops as you like," Bryn gushed, her mouth full with the last bite of fudge. "I never get to come to town and I so love it here."

She studied, with joy and wonder, the details of each building we walked by. To her, McLeod was exciting and modern.

I wondered: if I looked where she looked with fresh eyes would my cynical perception change?

This town had grown in proportion with the number of settlers, but it was evident those choosing to live and make a living here enthusiastically created a foundation for what they believed to be a prosperous future.

Once we changed directions from commerce to residential, my mind shifted to Barnes; I owed him an explanation and I knew just where to find him.

Bryn didn't say a word when we stopped in front of the school. She remained silent when I took her hand and led her up the stairs and into the building. But she did gasp when I opened the door to the classroom.

To her young eyes, this was a magical array of desks, empty today, but on any other day, filled with children her own age.

"A very good morning to you both!" an ever effervescent voice greeted us as Master Barnes entered the classroom from another door.

"I hope we are not interrupting," I said as a young girl stepped out from behind him carrying a box much larger than she should have been carrying.

"Not at all, we were just finishing up. Weren't we, Master Barnes?" This little one beamed up at him as if he were a heavenly being.

"We are finished, Lizzie. I see you've brought along a delightful companion of your own." Barnes came forth and knelt on one knee, offering Bryn an introductory handshake. "Master Barnes, headmaster of this school. And what might your name be?"

Bryn looked up at me for permission. Receiving my nod, she quietly answered, "Bryn Wright."

"Well, I don't know what your education plans are, but I do hope you will someday—"

"I am so sorry for your loss!" Lizzie rushed in between Barnes and Bryn.

Bryn looked up at me, both of us bewildered by what Bryn had lost.

"My grandfather died too. But I don't even be-member him. He was dead before I even got born." Lizzie took Bryn's hand from Barnes's and looked at Bryn with as much empathy as a young child might express.

I was witnessing Lizzie's repetition of what she had watched adults do. She was like an actress repeating her lines. Once I understood what Lizzie was doing, I knew what she was implying.

Barnes was brilliant in so many ways and equally smooth with his transitions. I wasn't sure what he saw in my expression, but it was enough to change the conversation with the children. "What is it I can do for my prairie—"

"Could we go out to play?" Lizzie interrupted, clearly as enraptured with Bryn as Barnes was with me.

"I can see one of the things we shall work on is waiting until one person is finished speaking before—"

"Could I?" Bryn interrupted, pleading for me to approve.

Barnes and I laughed. It was a perfect time to change the subject.

"Just for a short while," I agreed and they skipped out the same door from which Barnes arrived hand in hand.

"Why are children so naturally connected to one another at this age, but when they become adults, they'll not even share the same space with each other?" I asked.

"That is a long explanation for another day," Barnes said and escorted me to the front steps.

We sat under the shaded roof covering the top step.

"You didn't seem shocked by Lizzie suggesting my father is Bryn's grandfather." I watched Barnes carefully.

"There are several stories that have been shared about a number of families," he said diplomatically.

"But any as scandalous as my illegitimate daughter?" I asked, getting right to the point.

He paused, honestly considering his answer.

"I've witnessed a great many stories in my travels. Some true, most not. While I don't know you well, my Prairie Princess, I do know any daughter of yours would not be a secret," he said, reminding me once again why I admired him.

I was touched.

"All you need to know is Bryn's mother is an extraordinary woman. And a teacher, as my mother was before she died. How the rumor came to be is something I have not and will not discuss."

Barnes nodded and then changed the subject with a bit of humor. "Did you leave before midnight for fear of turning into a pumpkin?"

"I apologize for leaving without seeing you." I took a deep breath, hoping in the pause I might be able to explain myself.

"If I may." He waited for me to nod, giving him permission to answer his own question. "I noticed your leaving coincided with Beth's introduction to a lovely young woman named Anne?"

What was it about the easy way we communicated? He was observant of far more details than what appeared on the surface.

"And, I may add, you do have a way of looking at that attractive man in uniform," Barnes said, now trying to read my face or predict my response.

"That handsome man is a good friend," I said. Hearing the falseness in my own voice, I paused. "I'm realizing that handsome man that was once a good friend might be something else."

"As I thought." He patted my hand. "And I'm more than a little disappointed. Dare I wish for a glimmer of hope? It seems his dear mother was intent on announcing, however subtly, an upcoming engagement?"

"She was. But I wonder if it was to put me in my place?" I asked myself more than I was asking Barnes.

"You do have scars of the heart, though I know not the details." Barnes pulled his hand away creating a supportive space between us. "My sister had a similar look, and I knew the details of her scars."

His revelation was honest and dark, like the details of my scars.

Neither of which would be discussed further.

Barnes changed the subject. "I've confided there is another reason why I've come to this place. My plan is to begin as a school headmaster, but I wish to carve a different place for myself, in a business that doesn't yet exist, and it won't, until I'm known as the name behind that business."

"Will you share—" my question was blocked by a piercing scream coming from behind the building.

Bryn.

I'd completely forgotten about her being outside.

Truthfully? I'd completely forgotten about her all together.

Barnes and I were on our feet and down the stairs at the same time, both racing towards the sound.

As we rounded the building, we were met with an eerie silence. After such a visceral call for help, silence was not what I wanted to hear. Worse, there was no sign of either of the girls until Bryn's head lifted.

"Hannah!" she called.

No wonder I didn't see them, they were hidden in a thick cluster of weeping willow bushes. Once I was beside Bryn,

I was disturbed to see Sun Eagle standing a short distance away, as well as three boys, all older than Bryn, standing sheepishly silent.

Lizzie was lying at Bryn's knees, looking like she was in a dreamy sleep, but the grass beneath her head was darkening with the flow of blood. Surrounding her were three large rocks.

"Boys, what—" Barnes started.

"Hannah!" And there he was. Again.

Sam seemed always to be a short time and distance away from me, very often showing up when I needed him the most. He knelt to have a closer look at Lizzie.

"He did it," one of the boys finally spoke. Judging by the adolescent boy-man voice, it was likely the oldest of the trio. He was pointing at Sun Eagle.

Sam looked at Bryn for confirmation, but she was oblivious to everything except what she saw above her head. She was peacefully nodding her head as if in some conversation with someone only she could see.

I wrapped my arms around her without interrupting this trance-like behavior.

"Barnes, take Lizzie inside. William, go find your father. Jeffery, run to Dr. Patterson; I just saw him leaving the barracks. Hannah, take Bryn home." Sam's expression and tone told me all I needed to know.

Protect Bryn and Ivy.

Another Layer

MUCH AS I would have preferred to wait on the porch for Sam, it was too cool a night, and no matter what we did, we could not stop Bryn from trembling. Ivy and Bryn lay wrapped in a large blanket on a bed that was pulled in front of the fireplace. While the room looked cozy, not one of us felt comfortable.

When Bryn finally fell asleep, Ivy and I tiptoed to the table—close enough to keep a watchful eye on Bryn, but far enough to talk without her eavesdropping.

"What on earth would Sun Eagle be doing there?" Ivy asked quietly. "Time and time again, we asked that he release himself from protecting us. But he couldn't. He vowed when Night Star was murdered to protect me, and then to protect his sister. It sometimes felt like a nuisance; now it feels sinister."

"I hope Sam's protection will be enough for him," I said. While I had no feelings of kindness for Sun Eagle, I knew he would not throw a rock at a helpless child.

As if on cue, as so frequently occurred, I heard what I assumed to be Sam riding towards the house.

Ivy and I slipped outside and onto the porch.

Sam dismounted and took off his hat. The news was not good.

"Lizzie died from her injuries." Sam's voice sounded vacant of emotion. "Sun Eagle has been charged and we're holding him until we can investigate further."

"There is no way Sun Eagle—" I said, angry that Sam permitted juvenile detectives solve his case.

"There's no way we can prove otherwise at this point. Three witnesses say they saw the same thing: Sun Eagle hitting Lizzie with a rock," Sam clarified what we already knew.

"Witnesses who are too young to think for themselves," I hissed.

"Hannah, you and I are not judge and jury. There's a process. I'll do what I can to ensure it's fair." Sam sounded fatigued, but also irritated with me.

"How is Bryn?" Sam asked.

"She's finally asleep," Ivy answered, her concern superseding the fatigue on her own face. "We so hoped this land of the First People and the land of your father's would inspire our neighbors to live together differently. Tragic—when children bear witness to such acts of violence among themselves."

What could Sam or I say?

It was true. Children were at the very center of this tragedy.

"Ivy, if you are okay, I'd like to take a walk with Hannah?" Sam asked. He extended his hand towards me, but it sounded more instructional than invitational.

"Of course." Ivy stood and opened the door. "Hannah, it is time we show you the rest of the property. Tomorrow? It'll be a good distraction for Bryn."

That was the first time I'd heard her authority. She was also being more instructional than invitational. Strong, but gentle.

I was staying indefinitely, or until Sun Eagle was released, giving Ivy time to make better use of me. Clearly, there was work to be done.

Sam took my hand, but instead of leading me on a walk, he led me to the guest house.

Once inside, he went to work building a fire. I waited, wanting him to start the conversation he'd initiated.

"There were many times when I sat here with Thomas. Before and after his illness. I admired his mind, his vision and his leadership," Sam reminisced, still with his back to me.

Not the topic I was hoping for, and I certainly didn't have anything to add, given my admiration for him was nonexistent.

"He asked me to be the one to bring you home when he died." Sam turned now to face me. "And he asked, when I felt the time was right, that I tell you what he learned regarding Night Star's death."

I was trapped.

If I left, I would not be supporting Sam, who in turn needed to support Sun Eagle.

If I stayed, I would be facing details from a night I spent years trying to block from my mind and from my body.

I stayed.

"One of the persistent reports was that two traders came upon you being raped by two men: Night Star and another." Sam's voice was flat and procedural. "When they intervened to assist you, a dispute resulted in one man fleeing and Night Star being killed when he tried to attack the two traders."

Sam added more wood to the fire. "When two of these men brought you home, they were intent on having all their criminal charges dropped before they returned to Montana. The terms were simple: Colonel Wright drops the charges, they say nothing about what happened to you, thus preserving your honor. He reluctantly agreed, thinking these two were better off the other side of the border."

"Doesn't sound like great leadership to me," I said defensively. Where those words came from, I have no idea. I felt like I was outside my body listening to this conversation like an observer.

"Much as he regretted it later, he dropped their charges, but they proceeded to tell the tale in all the towns they travelled through before reaching Fort Benton. The story came back to him right around the time he was finalizing the treaty signing." Sam came and sat near me. "He sent you away to save you. You stayed away to punish him."

It was an oversimplification considering Sam had no idea what happened that night.

"The problem became much worse four weeks later when they found two other bodies downstream." He hesitated. "One of them was Morning Owl. The other—my father, Oliver Peters. Neither died of drowning."

I was stunned. My mind was racing as the questions surfaced at a speed much faster than I could ask them. "You said your father died when you were an infant." I settled on Oliver Peters.

Sam took a long pause. "My mother told me he died. This body had been dead for weeks…not thirty years!"

"Why would—"

Sam interrupted what he anticipated as my question. "I suppose in my mother's eyes, it was true. In her mind, he was dead," he said, shrugging.

"Your mother knew your father was alive?" I asked, stunned that Beth was capable of such deception.

"I don't have all the details, but I do know my father was addicted to two things: gambling and prospecting for gold. Those alone likely made him unsuitable as a husband or a father," Sam said, settling into another long pause.

"The other, maybe real problem? He was unofficially married to a Peigan woman. They had three children." Sam took my hand. "Based on what I know, he had no idea I existed. Obviously, there's a lot I don't know about him, but I do know he was there when Night Star was murdered. He was a lot of things, Hannah. Not one of them violent. I'm confident he was not a rapist. And, as we already know, neither was Night Star."

"Does Ivy know about Morning Owl?" I asked, turning the conversation away from me.

"She does. We both have a lot of unanswered questions," Sam said, releasing my hand and walking to the door. "I can't imagine what you experienced that night, but I can ask you to think about telling your side of the story. The only side of the story that is the truth."

And then he left.

The weight of Sam's challenge was oppressive for so many reasons, all of which added more devastation to an already calamitous series of events.

I curled onto my side and watched the fire burn itself out.

THE ONLY HUMAN *sound I heard was that of humans being entertained. The source of their entertainment: beating Night Star to death.*

I was still pinned under the body of this stranger, numb to what he had in store for me, when he whispered, "Be still and you will be safe."

I stayed still, but couldn't block the sound of Night Star's beating.

He lowered his mouth to my other ear. "I know what they are capable of. I've witnessed it. All I can do is protect you by keeping you silent."

Then he grabbed me, pulled me by the hair to my feet and dragged me toward Night Star.

"Looks like we all got ourselves a bit of entertainment!" That familiar menacing voice as he took a step towards me. "Not your usual preference. Maybe I should have a sample?"

"Not if you want to make a deal with Wright." He handed me a blanket and nodded in my direction. "His daughter will make for a fine exit south. For you both."

I found myself astride a horse with Night Star's battered body draped in front of me heading for home.

Life as I knew it was over.

A Glimpse of Wonder

GIVEN THE DAWN'S light, I anticipated Ivy's knock on my door, but I remained exactly as I was when Sam left me, still trying to wrap my head around his summation.

I did everything within my power to not think or remember or discuss what happened to me.

I never once thought about who the men were, where they came from or what was to be gained by their actions.

I was oblivious to the fact only two men brought me home.

All I could think about was my cowardice; my inability to speak or move or do anything but listen to Night Star's life evaporate with each stroke of violence.

By stepping forward, he sacrificed his life for my survival.

Ivy didn't knock, she entered quietly, dressed for the ride she proposed last night.

"It's a bit of a long ride today," she said.

Then she left, closing the door behind her. It was all business.

The horses were ready, not with the usual saddle blankets, but with three saddles. I couldn't remember the last time I rode western style with stirrups.

Bryn was usually euphoric when she sat upon Han. Today her face was without expression.

In one single moment, she was transformed from being innocently enthusiastic about all she encountered to having that shaded view of what was in front of her.

Still, she managed a weak smile when our eyes met.

Ivy joined us with the last of her gear, two heavily packed pairs of saddle bags.

Ivy led the way, Bryn in the middle, Jack settling into his role at the back.

I was unnerved by Ivy and Bryn's silence—that was usually my style.

The scenery is what became a welcome distraction. Surrounding me was a reminder of why so many settlers from easterly parts of this country and other countries oceans away sacrificed so much to build a new life here.

First, there was the space, at least where we were travelling, unoccupied and untouched.

Second, perhaps most significantly, the possibility of owning land to grow a family or whatever crops were hardy enough to survive.

I found myself comforted again by the Rocky Mountain silhouettes, although these mountain peaks were not snow-covered.

In fact, there was no evidence of snow anywhere. Already, the air and the vegetation showed more signs of summer than of spring.

Eventually, Ivy led us to a clearing surrounded by trembling aspens on one side, a slow-moving creek on the other and a trail descending to some place beyond my view.

She dismounted. Bryn and I followed, then secured the reins with enough lead for all three horses to drink and graze.

With a quick opening of a blanket, a simple lunch was presented. I remembered I hadn't eaten since breakfast yesterday. Still, no words were exchanged.

When we finished, Bryn lay her head on Ivy's lap. I had no capacity to address what she needed or to offer comfort. All Bryn needed was to know her mother was there.

"We will follow a path leading us from the edge of The Preservation to the beginning of the land of the First People," Ivy said, lightly stroking Bryn's forehead. "There are myths and stories telling of how the First People came to live here. The simplest? The land called the people hundreds of years ago. They were here before any of the nations now known as of the Blackfoot Confederacy, or the traders or the settlers."

I nodded.

"Those early people were not nomadic. They settled in an area with gentle seasons, abundant fishing, hunting and rich soil for planting. At first, they built small earth domes for shelter and relied more on what they grew or hunted than following the buffalo," Ivy continued, obviously wanting me to have more background before seeing the village.

"What might surprise you most is the others who have settled here." Ivy looked towards the valley.

"Your father and your grandfather were part of the solution to settle the land for the railway and settlers, but also to assist the struggling nations who were starving and homeless. With some negotiation, Paul drafted the legal document exempting the First People from the treaty signing. This exemption ensured the land was not only designated for the First People, but the First People owned the land."

Bryn sat up, looking at Ivy like her mother was saying something she had never heard before.

We were both more than intrigued.

I wondered if my face looked as awestruck as I felt, learning of my grandfather's legal involvement with the First People for the first time.

"There were also many who travelled great distances and suffered extreme hardships, but could not fulfill the expectation of working the land for three years. This is a challenging land, not a magical land. Those promoting the sale and settlement of land were dishonest with their promises. They were also dishonest with their presentation of the treaties."

Ivy started to repack the leftovers, continuing, "With time, the First People learned to speak the same Algonquin language, plus English and Spanish."

She paused as if considering what she was about to say. "As I speak I realize how so many other nations valued horses, guns and sadly, whiskey. But truly? Power exists when the language spoken is the language understood—we spoke the same language as business; then we learned how to become even more self-sufficient in the ways of business."

Bryn and I listened as we gathered our horses.

"While promoters of a new land painted an untrue picture, the First People saw the land for what it was and adapted to what the land yielded," Ivy finished and assisted Bryn onto Han.

I had at least a dozen questions, but Ivy had this way of speaking when she deemed the time right.

No more, no less. She was finished with providing the background.

The path down the hillside was impressively groomed, illustrating many hooves, wheels and feet had been on the same journey.

Giving Jack the reins, so to speak, I was in a better position to watch the trail in front.

In front of me was an aerial view of the First People village blueprint.

What struck me was the formation.

Most settlements were built on a grid of intersecting and connecting street lines. This settlement resembled an intricate spider web; aside from two long structures at the center, the surrounding dwellings were smaller and closer together.

As the village expanded, growing outwards north, east and south, the division of land became larger, more suited to ranching or farming.

When we entered the village, I could study it with more detail. The newer homes were indeed made of wood, the exteriors uniquely showcasing simple architectural preferences of the owners. One property contained a small herd of sheep in a small pasture surrounded by a barbwire fence. Another, an impressive assortment of beehives; still others surrounded by gardens newly planted with crops yet to be revealed.

I suspected we were heading towards the large, long wooden structures, but I was mesmerized as we passed the earth domes, as Ivy had described, blending in with the ground upon which they were constructed. It was a clever and resourceful concept that withstood the test of time.

The closer we got to the center longhouse, I noticed less of architecture and more of those living here. This village was a fusion of people: a blend of First People and people from other locations well beyond here. It was a beautiful assortment of skin and hair color.

Ivy stopped in front of the largest longhouse and dismounted.

An elder, the same elder who tried to barter with Randy when I first arrived in McLeod, stepped forward to greet her. White Feather wrapped his arms around her, then stepped away from her embrace, keeping a tight grip on her hands.

"What will we do now?" he asked.

"We will find a solution. As we always do." Ivy released her hands just as Bryn wrapped her arms around White Feather's waist and wept. He gently picked her up, cradled her lovingly in his arms and stepped inside.

"Come," Ivy said and offered me her hand. "Let me show you our gathering place."

The space inside was more impressive than the view from above. Constructed with large timbers, the interior was organized into open sections. While I was curious to examine the spaces with more detail, Ivy led us to a hearth where White Feather sat with Bryn.

Ivy and I settled on the wood floor, each with a sheepskin rug.

"Hannah, welcome to our village," White Feather spoke softly over Bryn's head in perfect English. "I feel compelled to apologize for Sun Eagle. He is passionate, but also impulsive and has been since we adopted him as a young boy. Now his reputation puts his actions in a precarious situation."

I was distracted again by the contrast. This was not the submissive elder trader I first witnessed at Clarkson's. This was a wise, powerful and compassionate man.

"Hannah," Ivy said, helping me to refocus. "As you noticed, parts of the village have been here for some time. You saw how the traditions and the innovations have fused together in a village. We would not be as we are without the help of your grandfather and your father."

"This land is secure. The issue now is who will own the land that belonged to your father." White Feather redirected us back to the most pressing issue. "Ivy will not be able to assume ownership; this your father and grandfather have confirmed. Not because she is a woman. But because, through marriage to my son, Morning Owl, she is a woman of the First People."

"But if I assume ownership—" I couldn't believe those words came from my mouth.

"And you agree with the vision we have created." White Feather observed my hesitance.

"You must want to assume your father's role, Hannah," Ivy added. "If you sell the land that is now yours, we will work with what we have. Until the new owner moves to claim what is being coveted."

There was a pause, maybe they were waiting for me to guess? I didn't have a clue.

"Coal." White Feather pointed in a direction behind him. Westerly, if we were standing outside the house.

I knew this was to be the fuel of the future. The fuel of innovation and development.

"We appreciate the resources nature provides. But mining for coal will weaken the mountain," Ivy spoke, stronger and with more conviction than White Feather. "And as the Chief of the First People, I will do what I need to do to ensure the mountains remain as the creator intended."

To my knowledge, chiefs were male. "As Chief of the First People?" I had to ask.

"This is another difference with our nation," White Feather chuckled.

"As the widow of the past chief, I assume that role until I marry or die," Ivy clarified.

"That is why you didn't marry my father," I reflected, thinking this to be brilliant on so many levels.

"Ours was a bond of souls, destined to lead the First People until the next chief is chosen. I am allowed and encouraged to marry, but when I do, a new chief is declared." Ivy nodded and took Bryn's hand. "When the time comes, if my life unfolds as I wish, Bryn will assume the role of chief. If she declines, the First People will go through a process of naming a new family lineage to determine their next chief."

Bryn, still cradled by White Feather, remained uncharacteristically quiet.

With more questions than answers, I followed Ivy on a walking tour.

"We only have a short time before we need to head back, but I do want you to understand how we share the land," she said as we exited from a different door.

She stopped a few steps from the longhouse and pointed north. "There is much valuable land in that direction. We have yet to determine how to share the forest's riches with those wishing to transform the trees into a railroad timbers for the north-south railway. Such a connection would strengthen our ability to trade."

She pointed east. "All the small homes you see over there? Those are leased sections of land. These are the homes of the settlers who near perished after the killing winter. Most can't pay their lease with money, so they trade what they make, grow or butcher. Some may never leave; some are close to paying for their own land not far from here."

In my travels from Fort McLeod to Toronto back to Calgary and then McLeod, I had not seen such creative land sharing ideas. So much of the settlement and growth patterns I had known were dependent on wealth, connections and a significant dose of good luck.

"How is it the First People remained conflict-free with other nations?" I asked.

"There is a deep understanding of the roots of this nation. The people who hunted and settled here first were not settlers, traders or explorers. They were people related to people who learned to survive and adapt on this vast land."

"Pretty close to a miracle based on what I've seen," I said.

In my opinion, humans seemed to always manage to ruin a good thing. "How is it you are so loved and accepted by a nation that is not part of your roots?"

"That is a story to be shared. Soon," Ivy promised. She wasn't avoiding my question; she was keeping an eye on the remaining hours of daylight. "It is time to return. To our home."

It was her home.

Ivy's and Bryn's.

Time for me to determine what role I would play to ensure it stayed that way.

For as long as they wished it to be so.

Towards the Truth

I T WAS DARK by the time we entered the gates, but there was light coming from the house. "Should we be worried?" I asked, easing Jack to a stop.

Ivy laughed. "It is funny how you have yet to actually see who helps me run the property on this side. There is no way I could do this on my own," Ivy said, nudging her horse onwards. "I do have two families that live close to the house. They help with the livestock and our house. Let me introduce you once the horses are settled."

Bryn and I took the horses to the small barn and relieved them of their harnesses and saddles. After a light brushing and surface cleaning of their hooves, we left them relaxed and content with fresh buckets of hay.

"Why do humans hurt each other?" Bryn's voice startled me.

Ivy and I had included her in the conversations today, but she had very little to say. This was the first time her words hinted at what she was processing.

"Good question," I said, continuing to walk towards the house. "I truly don't know what causes one human to want to harm another."

I spoke the truth, stalling a bit.

"Sun Eagle did not throw any rocks," Bryn said. She stopped and looked at me in earnest. "He often seems cross, but he is kind in his soul."

Whether that was true or not, I certainly had seen him be much more than cross and I had yet to witness this kindness in his soul. I knew what Bryn said to be the truth: Sun Eagle would not have thrown a rock so dangerously close to Bryn and, more to the point, why would he throw rocks in the first place?

Such mean-spirited action seemed more like a childish thing to do.

"How do you feel about telling Sam?" I asked, testing Bryn's readiness.

"I would…but Lizzie doesn't want her brothers to get hurt," Bryn said, looking upwards as if to validate her message with someone I couldn't see.

"Did Lizzie say anything to you before she was—"

"She had already crossed over, but before she can rest, she's asked me to make sure her brothers are safe," Bryn said, interrupting my question by summarizing this conversation as if I had heard it too.

"We can get Sam to help us with that one," I suggested.

Bryn smiled and, if I read her face accurately, she was relieved to have a solution to her dilemma. "Let's go get something to eat," she said.

Slipping her hand in mine, we walked towards the house.

Bryn was asleep before Ivy pulled the quilted covers over her. Ivy studied her peaceful face as she swaddled Bryn into a protective quilted cocoon.

Once we were settled in front of the fire with a clear view of Bryn sleeping, I felt compelled to share my conversation with Bryn.

"Bryn mentioned something unusual." I watched the fire as I spoke cautiously. "She's concerned about observing Lizzie's wish to protect her brothers."

"Did she have this conversation with Lizzie before she lost consciousness?" Ivy asked.

I shook my head and clarified, "She speaks as if she communicated with Lizzie after she died."

Ivy nodded. "Bryn has a gift. The gift of being able to connect to the space between a person's death and their arrival to their afterlife," Ivy said, watching my reaction intensely. "This gift…she inherited from her father, Morning Owl. We call them spirit walkers."

If I was being honest with myself, the concept made me feel uneasy. I felt compelled to share my concern. "It wasn't that long ago females were labelled as evil spirits or witches for uttering such things," I said, now watching Ivy's reaction intensely. "I'm not so sure that dangerous time is truly in the past," I added.

Ivy nodded. "True. Talk of spirit walkers would not be understood or appreciated, especially for those who align with the house of God."

It was slight, but there was a hint of sarcasm in her tone.

"The First People believe these spirit walkers are guides for both the dead and the living. Before Bryn was born, it was foretold she was one," Ivy said, standing to make sure Bryn was still asleep. "She has told me of meeting her father, Morning Owl," Ivy whispered and sat back down. "But he died the day she was born. The same day as Night Star."

"Sam told me about Morning Owl," I said.

Ivy sighed. "Those four weeks were—" Ivy stopped, like the breath was stolen from her effort to speak.

"It started that night. The night of Night Star's murder," Ivy continued. "Morning Owl woke from a nightmare, and then he knew it to be much worse. All he told me was he heard Night Star call his name. This was the first time I witnessed the power of spirits; I wasn't certain what it meant other than his abrupt departure. I tried to go back to sleep, but Bryn decided it was her time to be born," Ivy said, shaking her head. "When they placed her precious body in my arms, White Feather told me of Night Star's death." Ivy paused to check on Bryn. "It was a foreign space: euphoric joy for Bryn, devastating grief for Night Star."

My empathy for Ivy combined with my own experiences of devastation, giving me the sensation of sharing her memory. It was a heartbreaking space in time. for us both.

"It was weeks before Morning Owl's body was found. It was much longer than that for me to recover," Ivy said, looking at me. "Sam has more to discover himself. It seems we are surrounded by layers upon layers of tragedy—you, me and Sam."

Ivy reached for my hand. "We may learn more when you are ready to speak. In time, you will also know when to share your truth. While we wait, we accept what is."

Ivy stood. "It has been a long day. Sleep well, dear Hannah."

This would be the end of our conversation.

Conversation Starters

I SLIPPED OUT OF Ivy's door, fully intending to walk directly to the guest house. As soon as I took a deep breath of the night air, the pounding in my ears subsided. I kept walking.

I was worried about Bryn; I knew how violence had changed my life at a young age.

I wondered what role I would play in the future land Ivy had been instrumental in managing—while grieving the loss of three loves!

The majority never meet their first love, let alone marry and create a home and family. But Ivy did. Twice. The loss of her first son was a completely different love; one I doubt she will ever recover from. And now, Bryn was caught in the middle of a different loss—the senseless death of a child she had befriended.

There was no way I was going to sleep tonight.

Glancing upward, I determined there would be no moonlight to guide my ride back to McLeod. Any threat to my safety would appear without warning. But when had that ever stopped me before?

If I took Jack, Ivy would hear and likely stay awake worrying. She didn't need anything else to worry about.

Impulsively or instinctively, I continued walking away from the safety and security of Ivy's home.

It was time to interrupt the sleep of others who could help me resolve Sun Eagle's implication in Lizzie's death.

It seemed like no time had passed before the town came into my view. Plus, I wasn't on edge wondering if Sun Eagle would appear; I knew exactly where he was.

At least for now.

It did strike me as odd that her door was unlocked. Did she assume her namesake was a deterrent for those seeking harm to her person or her property?

Once inside, I followed the dim light coming from the kitchen.

She faced away, pouring hot water into a teapot, a teapot much too ornate for this hour.

"I guess you couldn't sleep either." Beth spoke as if she was addressing a restless child, but in a tone soft enough to reveal a hint of maternal instinct.

When she turned to face her guest, her expression remained unchanged, but I saw her body stiffen briefly.

She was startled and a bit frightened. She reset instantly, becoming her familiar rigid, cold self.

"Samuel will not return until the day after," Beth said, speaking as if I was doing business with him.

I had to admit, I was impressed that she could sound so authoritative despite my surprise entrance. I wasn't here to be dismissed. Maybe she sensed that; she held her stance.

It was at this precise moment I noticed how small she was.

In my mind, she always appeared tall and intimidating, yet here before me, wearing only her dressing gown and slippers, her power diminished. She was an old, cynical woman.

"You may have given up the Clarkson name when you married, but you still have authority," I said, blocking her exit to outside or an alternate location in the house.

"I have no idea what you are talking about," she said, taking a sip of tea as if we were discussing a change in the weather.

"Sun Eagle's word versus the word of a young Clarkson. One of your nephews," I said. There was no point dancing around what needed to be said.

"Hannah," she said, emphasizing her exasperation as if we'd been discussing this issue for years. "I may be of service to both church and school, but I most certainly do not interfere with the law," she said with a new tone, one of speaking to a simpleton.

Without the armor of her wardrobe, she was just a woman I was talking to. A woman unprepared for my next question.

"Did you interfere with the law when you fabricated your husband's death?" I asked.

Her demeanor changed. Was it shock, surprise or fear? Whatever she felt was irrelevant. She was visibly shaken, yet silently testing the validity of my accusation.

I knew I had her full attention, so I continued. "Many didn't realize he was alive while Sam was growing up. Most would never guess he was there when Night Star was murdered."

These two facts weakened her to her core. Not trusting the tea to stay in her teacup, or her ability to stand, she sat on the closest chair.

I hated to admit it—I had a moment of empathy for her.

"It may be a relief to know your husband had nothing to do with Night Star's murder, but he was with those two traders—for some reason other than seeking and killing a young man from one of the nations," I said, pausing for dramatic impact. "Now that is a detail the law would be most interested in exploring."

Beth took an unsettled sip of tea, then waited.

"The fact he was a witness to a crime, plus his other dealings away from McLeod, would tarnish the Clarksons' good name. But your biggest challenge is both the validity of your marriage and whether Sam was born with the Peters' namesake. What will have the most negative impact? Sam's mixed race half-siblings across the border."

In a few powerful phrases, I metaphorically pressed her against the wall with no room to escape the truth. I realized I was holding my breath and honestly, I felt a bit like a bully. I stood down in a sense, changing my position from blocking her exit to giving her an option.

She remained in place as I had hoped.

"You may think being silent in Lizzie's death helps you even the score. It only worsens it. Hatred leads to more hatred. It's learned not innate," I said, toning it down a bit more. "It was that learned hatred that motivated a young boy to use violence when he encountered someone with a different skin color than his own," I said. "All you need to do is speak with Randy. The two of you can change this outcome…you need to speak up or I will."

Then I left through the same door I had entered.

When I stepped outside, the fresh air seemed to neutralize the tension that was building since my return to McLeod. While the myths of my reputation were an ongoing source of McLeod gossip, I used facts as a weapon to motivate Beth to speak up. It was better to be a widow than to acquire the reputation of an unwed mother, now with an adult son with an illegal last name.

As I walked away I realized I was muted by the trauma of surviving that night; I never imagined something positive could come from any of the details I allowed myself to remember.

As I approached the barrack's guardhouse, it appeared serene. I assumed it was partly due to the late hour and partly due to the town's focus on preparations for Lizzie's funeral. Once inside, I walked towards the desk. There was only one Mountie, although in uniform, he appeared far too young to be left in charge for the evening.

Beyond him were four jail cells with only one occupied.

Whereas Beth acted as if she was not in the least bit surprised to see me, this young corporal tripped over his feet, which had been resting unprofessionally on the desk, and walked towards me still half asleep.

"Madame. Are you hurt?" he asked, genuinely concerned as he assessed my being.

It was a natural guess. Why else would I be here at this hour?

"Yes, I'm fine," I assured him. "My name is Hannah Wright. Colonel Thomas Wright's daughter."

It was a night of what I might call 'never imagines'—using my father's name to gain advantage was yet another surprise. The mere mention of his name and my relationship inspired the corporal to stand as if the Colonel was right beside me.

"I am sorry for your loss. He was a great man," he said, lowering his hat to his chest.

"Thank you." I spoke in a respectful tone. "I wish to speak with one of your inmates."

"That would not be advisable, Madame," he said, placing his hat back on his head.

This might not be as easy as it first seemed. My next option was to continue throwing around names until one gave me a pass.

"I just came from Madame Peters. She will be stopping by to discuss new information in the morning. She asked that I speak with Sun Eagle before she arrives," I said, sounding as truthfully official as possible.

"You may see him," he said, uncomfortable with his decision. "But for only a few minutes."

He stepped aside, clearing a path for me to walk towards Sun Eagle's cell.

Sun Eagle had the appearance of resting on the narrow cot—his head towards the bars, his feet toward the farthest cell wall. His eyes were wide open, gazing at the ceiling. I knew, given his proximity to my conversation, he heard every word I said and still he acted like I wasn't there.

"I know you can hear me," I said. Even though logistically the iron bars separated us, I was still intimidated by him. "The one thing we share in common is hatred for me. For my being there when Night Star was killed," I said, speaking in a language he would listen to. The language of revenge.

Something in his aloof demeanor shifted.

Whatever it was, I didn't care.

I needed to say what I needed to say. "The difference between the hatred you and I feel is… I hate myself more than you could ever possibly hate me."

He turned his head.

It was one of those moments.

"I will hate myself until I take my last breath. You can too. But for now, Bryn needs you to be a witness to what happened. To not let hatred silence you as it has silenced me."

He looked away, but I knew he was still listening.

"The rock was intended for you. Not Lizzie. Not Bryn," I said, giving him the quick facts. "Someone will change the charges. All you need to do is tell the truth. About what you saw and why you were there in the first place."

I turned away, nodding my gratitude to the corporal as I walked back out the door.

It was the first time Sun Eagle and I had the same job to do: wait until the morning.

It was an unreasonable time to be roaming around McLeod; even the saloon was closed for the night. But there was one light on, indicating someone else was awake at Clarkson's Mercantile.

My guess? Randolph Clarkson Junior.

I could hear him before I could see him, smashing something about in the supply room. Given the racket, he wouldn't hear me if I knocked on the locked front door. I followed my previous path at the side of the store.

When he did come into my sight, I noticed he was perspiring beyond normal. Not knowing his state of mind, I didn't want to startle him by simply appearing, so I whistled before speaking. "Randy?"

The whistle worked; he stopped and looked my way.

His face was expressionless—I knew the look; grief so deep words could never describe.

I noticed piles of dry goods in need of unpacking for inventory. The pattern was easy to identify. I started to help him unpack, then handed the first item, a bag of flour, to Randy for his inventory ledger.

At first, he looked at me like I had lost my senses. I looked right back at him, willing him to just keep working.

And work we did, silently until dawn.

With the last item logged for the store, Randy closed his ledger, lowered his head to his hands and wept. I sat beside him and waited.

When he lifted his head, he cleared his nose and eyes with an already well-used handkerchief, and spoke for the first time since I arrived. "She was our only girl. Five children, but only one girl."

"I only met her once," I said, keeping my voice low and calm. "She was kind and generous to my only sister."

"She was kind and generous to every living thing," Randy continued, anger adding bitterness to his sorrow. "Look where that got her."

What could I say?

It got her in the middle of a rock intended for Sun Eagle.

I doubted Beth had made her way to the barracks yet, but I felt it crucial that Randy know what I knew.

"The boys weren't aiming for Lizzie or Bryn. They were aiming at Sun Eagle, one of the First People trying to trade goods at your store," I said, gently reminding him of the business only a few days ago.

Randy had lost track of time and wasn't putting my vague details together on his own.

"Beth is on her way to clear Sun Eagle from the boys' allegations," I continued, watching Randy, still unsure where his fury and grief would lead him.

"But they said he threw the rocks." Randy's anger was still audible, denial becoming a welcome distraction. Randy knew his aunt would not be doing what I said she was doing without cause.

"They lied," I said, hearing the change in my own voice. Now I was angry. "They lied to protect themselves. They blamed the person most likely to be assumed guilty without the truth being told."

Randy shook his head. "Two of those boys were her brothers."

No wonder denial brought him comfort. I wondered if there could be a more challenging position for a parent. It was a bitter dilemma.

"My family can't change what happened. But we can be there when you need us." I stood. "And you will need us."

While I had very little respect for Randy, I did feel more than a little sorry for him.

I also felt hopeful.

This was the first time in his life when the Clarkson name would not shift the scales of fairness.

Time to Remember

As I approached The Preservation with the rising sun, I saw the incredible beauty of the property in a different light. It was breathtaking from the perspective of nature alone. For those paying attention, the amount of potential wealth and prosperity simmering within the property would take any investor's breath away.

Despite the splendor, I was confident this would not be my home; however, I could play whatever role was needed to ensure Ivy and Bryn and those living off or leasing the land could call it their home if they elected to do so.

As much as I wished otherwise, Lizzie's death would not change the pattern of racial mistrust in the town of McLeod, but I knew it did change something within Randy. Whatever that was would still be insignificant.

I needed someone with enough clout to help me on a much larger, legal scale. And I knew exactly who that person would be.

When I entered the house, I was surprised to find Ivy and Bryn preparing a travel lunch.

"You are just in time." Ivy's smile was weary, but cheerful for Bryn's sake.

"We were going to wait for you," Bryn said, rushing over to wrap her loving arms around me.

"Are you heading back to the village?" I asked.

"Not the village…I'd like to show you a different part of the property, and the weather agrees," Ivy said, turning to Bryn. "Are your chores are finished?"

She nodded her head.

"Can you go help saddle our horses?" Ivy asked.

Any request that involved Bryn riding Han was joyfully fulfilled. With Bryn gone, Ivy turned her attention to me.

"You are an adult, so I don't need to check where you sleep or when you come or go—"

"But you would like me to let you know, so you don't worry about me," I interrupted, feeling bad that my absence caused her unnecessary stress; Ivy was not familiar with my habitual disappearing acts.

She smiled and handed me one of the panniers as we stepped outside.

"This vista never disappoints," she said, taking in the view in almost the same way I did just a few moments ago.

"We have a lot to deal with, but I am curious…how is it you travelled such a distance to call this place home?" I asked. I had been longing to know Ivy's story since I first saw the family photo. That interest was becoming slightly obsessive with each tiny nugget she shared.

"In short, my father aspired be the first to distill spirits in Fort McLeod. He'd been doing so in several locations south of here. To ensure his business plan was successful, he also arranged for me to marry me to an influential man from a well-established family," Ivy said, pausing to look at me before continuing. "The Peters family."

I'll admit, the new information I'd learned in the last forty-eight hours was substantial, but this was riveting.

I had to clarify. "Oliver Peters?"

Ivy nodded. "I learned some time after that Oliver married Beth Clarkson," she said.

"Your mother agreed to this arranged marriage?" I asked.

Ivy smiled as if remembering a private joke. "My mother remained in St. Louis. Her marriage to my father was arranged, so she embraced me following in her footsteps… something Bryn will not be doing!" she added for emphasis. "We travelled by steamboat, oxen coach and then stage coach. The closer I got to Fort McLeod, the less I wanted to return to my home. The less I wanted to go home, the more I realized the importance of choosing my own husband."

I heard Bryn approaching the house, so I pressed for a few more details. "How did the marriage plan shift so dramatically from Oliver to Morning Owl?"

Ivy chuckled.

"I snuck into my father's first meeting with the First People as well as many chiefs from other nations. I was mesmerized by the language." Ivy turned to me. "The First People were fluent in English and not as inclined to get involved with the trading—which was always strategically designed to profit those wanting to settle the region, not those who called this their home."

Ivy stopped moving. "Do you believe it possible to recognize the soul of your heart when you meet that person?" Ivy asked.

Too much had happened for me to ever be aware of another person in such an intimate way. I shook my head.

"I didn't either. Until I met Morning Owl. My soul knew instantly what he would become. And I would do anything to speed up the process." Ivy stepped out the door, motioning for me to follow. "We were joined two days later. I lost my birth family when I became the wife of the future chief of the First People. Now they are my family. Thomas became my second family. And now we have you, whether you stay or go."

I was touched. First that she shared her story, and second that she had the capacity to speak of emotions so significant despite all she'd lost.

Emotions I had not, to this point, felt.

A ride would do us all good today.

I had travelled west, south and north, but not east of The Preservation.

While I had been attentive to the land around me earlier, I was deep in my own thoughts, vacillating between Ivy's true love story and the additional mystery of Morning Owl and Sam's father. Perhaps the most heartfelt distraction was reconciling how to adjust to belonging to Ivy and Bryn's family, knowing I would be leaving.

"Hannah, can you lead for a bit?" Ivy asked, bringing my attention back to the ride. She guided her horse aside, assuming my former position behind Bryn. "We're almost there."

The trail descended into thicker, intricately intertwined dwarf blueberry shrubs covered in tiny pink flowers promising a rich profusion of blueberries.

And then, almost as if it appeared out of nowhere, we were at the water's edge.

The place I vowed never to see again.

My mind reeled back in time, images that shouldn't be remembered replaced with what I saw before me.

Just as my heart started to race, Ivy nudged her horse to my right side and Bryn did the same at my left. They both looked at the water's edge serenely while I looked for a place to escape.

"We call this place Forget Me Not Pond," Ivy said, not to inform, but to capture my attention. "After Night Star died, the First People gathered here with his remains. Although there are still some of our people who fear the underwater, most now embrace the gifts of purification water provides."

"I love to come here to visit him," Bryn added.

"He was kind when he was a boy. He was maturing to become a peaceful man. A man who should have lived long enough to become chief of the First People," Ivy whispered, speaking openly about her first and only son.

She dismounted and Bryn followed.

Together, she went about the business of setting up the picnic.

To be honest, I felt a bit betrayed, like this was a set-up. Then my rational mind intervened with this pattern of destructive thinking. A mother and sister had come to remember Night Star: Ivy's son; Bryn's brother.

This was not about me; I could leave if I wanted, but for some reason I felt compelled to stay.

Once they were seated, looking out at the water, I dismounted and joined them. We sat silently, looking at the sun's reflection, listening to the waves caressing the shore.

"You may not recognize the water's edge…due to a great rainstorm weeks after he died. As the rivers swelled, the overflow created a larger pond. It's as if the place Night Star died has been cleansed by nature itself. It is a peaceful place. Very much like him," Ivy said.

She closed her eyes and lifted her head upwards. "We choose to remember and honor the man he was to become and the son he was," she said.

Two opposing emotions were at loggerheads inside me: I was frightened by my memories from a single moment in time and I was calmed by their memories of Night Star's short lifetime.

Despite this intensity, I could feel Bryn's energy building until she could hold her thoughts no longer.

"Will you ever find the words to tell your story?" she asked, sounding as wise as an elder.

"Bryn." Ivy's voice sounded like a warning.

"I know Madre, but—"

"I will tell my story, but not in the way others do," I promised, wrapping my arm around Bryn.

She accepted my offering by relaxing closer to me.

Time for a Change

I LAY AWAKE IN the room where my father took his last breath. This was the first time I'd thought about him as my father rather than a disappointment.

Like Ivy's, Thomas Wright's life had layers of losses: loss of his first wife, loss of his daughter, loss of his sense of law and order and loss of direction. If I lowered my defensiveness, I could understand how his concern for me clouded his better judgement. There are things in life that can't be fixed. Colonel Wright decided to think forward and, despite losing his eldest daughter, fix the future.

My thoughts returned to Ivy.

Whereas I became bitter and isolated because of my experiences, she faced her sorrow and took assertive measures to preserve all that she valued with more intensity and strength than ever before. Were people born with that capacity or did they learn it through life itself?

The fact I was even having this conversation with myself illustrated the answer to my own question...leading to yet another question: how would I live differently if I stopped blocking opportunities for my future.

To do that, I needed to decide how I could preserve all that was precious to Ivy and Bryn.

If Beth was telling the truth, Sam should be arriving within the hour.

I took a seat outside the barracks. I knew Sun Eagle had been released, at least I hoped that was true, given the cells were as empty as was the corporal's desk.

Sam rode towards the stables, oblivious to the surroundings so familiar to him until he sensed he was not alone. Making eye contact with me, he signaled his horse to turn in my direction.

His smile told me all I needed to know.

Sam dismounted, secured the reins to a post and sat beside me.

"You've been busy," he said, leaning forward so his elbows were resting on the top of his legs.

I wasn't sure where business had taken him or the nature of that business. I knew he was quieter than usual. To get a better read on his demeanor, I reached for his elbow. It felt so good to be beside him. It always had.

"I have been busy," I said.

We sat in silence.

I was taking my time before speaking to assess, one more time privately, my decision to proceed with my new plan.

"I want to know if you'll escort me back to Paul's," I said, watching his expression. "He's the only one who can help me review the property transfer to ensure Ivy and Bryn never need to fear another claiming ownership of The Preservation."

He let out a sigh of relief. "This is exactly what Thomas wished for."

"He already has all the ledgers and affairs in good order, but Ivy's challenge is that she married the former chief of the First People and united with my father. Her unclear status makes her vulnerable to those who create land ownership laws."

"I have some lieu time owing and I can think of no better way to spend that time than escorting you back," Sam said, touching the top of my hand with his own.

"I'll meet you here tomorrow," I said, standing. And then I noticed Sam's unfamiliar smile. "What?" I asked for clarification.

"Nothing. Nothing all," Sam said and stood. "Until tomorrow."

I sat on the steps of the school assuming Barnes would venture outside just before the lunch hour, but he startled me by rushing towards the school instead leaving the building. Clearly wrapped deeply in his own thoughts, he noticed a person sitting on the steps, but didn't take the extra time to focus on who it was.

"Excuse me, Madame," he said politely, taking the steps two at a time.

"Master Barnes!" I said. I wasn't going to let him get by without stopping to chat.

"My Prairie Princess," he said, pivoting and taking a seat beside me on the same stair. "I have been so worried, but I am now relieved to see you. What an alarming series of events since we last saw each other."

His voice had lost its joy and his coloring was unusually pale.

"Probably not part of what you envisioned as your responsibilities when you accepted this contract," I said.

"My dear, I have seen more violence than I care to remember in my travels, but it's true, I did not envision being responsible for seeking the truth when such violence involved children," Barnes said.

And there it was. What happened to me years ago seemed somehow worse in the context of Lizzie's death, because nothing had changed.

"I will stay on for at least the year in the hopes some good will emerge from such tragedy," Barnes said, shrugging his shoulders.

"They are fortunate to have you. When your year is up, I may have a space for you to bring your idea to life," I said, patting his knee.

He looked at me. "You remembered."

"I did. And I will discuss this further when I return. But I need to leave for a couple of days," I said.

"With a handsome Mountie to protect you I hope." He winked.

"With a friend who happens to be a Mountie to keep me company," I reminded him. While I admitted to enjoying my moment with Sam, I was not comfortable discussing him with Barnes.

He stood and clasped both of my hands in his. "You are a breath of fresh air. Safe travels and I look very forward to discussing my plans for next year when you return."

Ever the gentleman, he lightly kissed the tops of both my hands and then took the steps one at a time into the school.

Home for Business

P AUL OPENED HIS front door long before we stood in front of his verandah. Watching his face as we approached, I recognized the look: curious yet relieved.

While our relationship was one of tremendous love, it was rare for either of us to demonstrate our mutual affection.

Once I dismounted and stood in front of him, Paul wrapped his arms around me and held me tight.

He released me from his embrace, placed his hands on my shoulders and stepped back to take a long look at me.

"How is my favorite granddaughter?" he asked.

"You mean your only granddaughter." I smiled. "I will be much better with your help."

"You've come to the right place," Paul said, his hand now reaching for Sam's

Sam shook Paul's hand. "Nice to see you, sir."

The three of us spent much of the remaining hours of daylight reviewing my father's books. There was not a lot of conversation until Paul finally removed his spectacles, his trademark gesture before sharing his summation.

"The smartest thing Ivy did was not marry Thomas," he said. "I know Thomas wanted to override her common sense, to show his commitment to her. But she was firm, knowing what must be done."

"I've been surprised by a great many things in the last few days. Like your involvement with The Preservation. With the relocation of families to the First People's village," I said, trying to look stern, folding my arms across my chest for further dramatic impact.

"Hannie," he said, using his charm, "I'm not making excuses, but Thomas was shattered when your mother died. He was out of focus for years. I think when he saw you with those traders, he felt responsible—like he failed as a parent and that left you vulnerable." Paul waited and watched my response. "You know he kept tabs on you, despite you doing everything in your power to repel his efforts. The more you refused to communicate, the stronger he became—his new focus was to protect the three women in his life."

There were still many issues I would need to deal with. Today was not the day for that kind of reflection or forgiveness.

"In the eyes of the law and the ways of the First People nation, Ivy is the widow of the former Chief and thus remains so until she marries or her daughter assumes the role," I said.

"I have a lot of respect for this nation—theirs is a society that gives power fairly to both males and females."

"And so, it seems, does your family," Paul said. "If you accept your inheritance, it could be in name only. You can also make it your home."

"I'm looking at the immediate future," I said, watching Sam's face. "I'm not certain of all the details, but I do know I will not call McLeod my home."

I wondered if Paul read something in Sam's body language, something I might have missed or if he was focused on the legal tasks at hand.

"The First People's rights to the land and the subsequent leasing agreements, are iron clad. With your name on The Preservation land title, Ivy and Bryn will continue living and making a living on The Preservation," Paul said and closed the remaining books, stacking them in chronological order.

"Hannah, you have a home here for as long as you like," he said and winked. "In fact, this will all be yours as well."

Paul stood and shook Sam's hand. "I have plenty of room for you as well."

Once Paul left, Sam and I looked at each other in a somewhat awkward silence, unsure if Paul was making some kind of proposal on Sam's behalf.

Then we both burst out laughing.

Uncontrollably.

To the point of near tears. Laughter works like a pressure relief valve.

I stood, took Sam's hand in mine and led him to the barber space.

Stretched before me, on my grandfather's well-worn chair, was a beautiful man. Although we were childhood friends, I realized I now cared for him in a way different from that of a friend.

He was long in his body. Although off-duty, he was respectfully dressed as a representative of the law. His face, showing some signs of age, usually clean shaven, had a shadow of growth that would, if left untouched, become a beard.

Relaxed assuredly in my loving hands, he closed his eyes. It was a moment of surrender, of trust and of being where he most wanted to be.

I reached across him for a moist towel and wrapped it around his face, gently pressing my palms along the edges of his jaw, the surfaces of his eyebrows and the ridges of his cheek bones.

The tools, all left in an orderly fashion, awaited.

Lifting the polished handle of the shaving brush, I tested the suppleness of the bristles, then removed the towel from Sam's face.

I moistened the brush, then meticulously swirled the brush with soap, inhaling the lilac fragrance before covering Sam's emerging beard with lather.

Pressing the blade to his neck, I scraped lather and stubble in smooth upward strokes. Dipping the whitened blade into the basin, I watched the freshly exposed skin pulse with the beating of his heart. Again, I made more lines of un-lathered skin, still watching the steady rhythm of his heart.

I continued until all the lather and whiskers had been lifted from his face.

Taking another moist towel, I lovingly touched every part of Sam's face.

"That was the best shave I have ever had." Sam sat up and took my hands in his.

"I've been taught by the best," I said, taking a moment to tidy up Paul's space, knowing there would likely be some unexpected traveler coming his way some time tomorrow.

I took Sam's hand in mine and led him to my house in the woods.

As predicted, the fireplace was ready, with plenty of wood to keep us warm for as long as we wished. I invited Sam to take a seat on the floor beside me.

"You were right," I said, lightly caressing the top of his hand. "Your father was not a rapist."

As much as I thought I was ready to tell my story, I felt the words stick, like I couldn't control my emotions.

"You don't have—" Sam offered.

"I do have to." I urged myself onwards. "I don't need to tell you the whole story, but I need to tell you that your father saved me from harm by simply asking me to stay silent."

Sam frowned. "Why would he want you to stay silent?"

"It wasn't his request to be silent that kept me silent. Don't you see?"

And then the tears emerged. Rather than dam the flow of emotion, I released it. The more the tears fell, the more I found my voice. "I have punished myself for my selfishness. I did nothing to save Night Star. I took your father's advice, but I wasn't silent to protect anyone. I was silent because I was ashamed. Ashamed of my cowardice."

Sam shifted our hand positions so he was now caressing the top of my hand, and he waited.

"Riding back with Night Star dead in front of me was horrific. Each step the horse took reminded me that he was more dead and I was more of a coward for being alive. When we faced my father, I was naked wrapped only in a blanket. Not because I had been raped. Not because I had been intimate with Night Star. We had simply met to swim by the light of the full moon," I said, my words flowing as freely as my tears.

I turned to look at Sam, knowing my face was a mess of tears and mucus. "Who would believe our adventure started out to be so innocent?"

And then I surrendered, curling into Sam's body in such a way as to force both of us to lay side by side on the floor, wrapped in a blanket until my tears stopped and we both fell asleep.

Beyond

PAUL STOOD BESIDE Jack and looked up at me. "Are you certain you need to go back so soon?"

"There is a funeral we need to attend, and then we must get these affairs in order," I said, patting the panier securing the will and my father's books.

"Sam, will you go with her to the McLeod solicitor I have suggested?" Paul asked Sam.

"He will be happy to finalize these affairs." Sam nodded.

"I'll be back soon," I said, realizing I had never made such a promise to Paul or to anyone.

As we rode away, Sam and I side by side, I also felt something I had never felt before—a touch of sorrow leaving my grandfather.

Strange, I'd escaped from his house and property so many times and never had I experienced this sensation; a feeling so strong, I felt compelled to look back.

He was standing exactly where I left him.

This ride back to McLeod was much faster than our last. Eager to please, the horses were invigorated by the speed. While we had hoped to attend Lizzie's funeral, we were confident we'd be back for the community gathering after.

As we approached Randy's house, it was evident the entire town had the same idea. The streets and sidewalks were buzzing with movement, some towards the house, others away from it and many more settling into the spaces in the yard. Knowing a short walk would be good for both of us, we left our horses a distance away.

I was so focused on readying myself to communicate my condolences, I didn't notice Ivy and Bryn walking towards us. It was Bryn who saw me first, breaking free from Ivy's hand and sprinting towards Sam and I.

Once she wrapped her arms around my waist, she was inconsolable; I simply knelt beside her and waited.

"How were you received?" Sam asked Ivy.

"A few sideways glances, but that was all," Ivy said, likely being generous in her summation.

Bryn finally released herself from my embrace and looked at me.

"I am sad for Lizzie's family, but don't they know she has gone to a happier place?" Bryn spoke about this happier place differently than most referenced heaven or the afterlife or whatever phrase people used to explain life after death.

We three adults stood still, waiting.

"She is at peace. Her brother is loved and protected, even though he made a mistake," Bryn said, using her sleeve to clear her face of tears. "Madre, when I grow up I might not become chief. I think I might want be a spirit walker for McLeod. Hannah, do you think I could do that?"

When I looked at her, so wise yet so young, I answered truthfully, "I think you can do whatever you decide to do."

Ivy took Bryn's hand. "We'll see you for a shared meal tonight," she said. "The both of you."

It was not an invitation. She knew we would be there.

While Sam and Bryn cleared the plates, Ivy lifted an ornate carafe with matching glasses to the table and proceeded to pour four glasses of an amber liquid, Bryn receiving the glass with the smallest pouring.

"Salud," Ivy said, raising her glass.

"To Hannah, the owner of The Preservation. To Bryn, the future chief of the First People or the future owner of The Preservation or McLeod Spirit Guide or all three," she said, laughing. "To Sam, champion for those in need of strength and guidance. And to Thomas, now truly at peace."

We all lightly touched each other's glasses, making eye contact to acknowledge the significance of Ivy's words and the acknowledgement that the future was secure.

"To Ivy, your strength and love of family is what binds and heals," I said, hearing the unevenness of my voice. "You were a gift to my father and for that I am grateful."

"To Sam and Hannah," Bryn said, breaking the seriousness with her lighthearted voice. "Madre, can a spirit guide also be a marriage talker?"

The entire table stopped moving.

Bryn giggled, connecting Sam's hand to mine, and turned her attention to the next item on her mind.

"Also, Master Barnes has invited me to join classes, but he is sorry for not being able to teach me Spanish," Bryn said, sipping her mead, and waited.

"You have a lot of plans. Let's take them one step at a time," Ivy said, helplessly looking at me over Bryn's head.

"Starting with the school. I think that sounds like a great idea. Especially, when Master Barnes is there," Sam said, shrugging and neatly dodging the topic of marriage.

We each took luxurious sips in silence…connected to each other because of our past, yet stronger together because of the work still to be done.

It was a solid and secure place to be.

Once Ivy and Bryn started their bedtime routine, Sam and I stepped outside. I sensed there was much on his mind; I knew it was more vague than what occupied mine.

"Once the papers are signed, you'll be free to head back to Paul's," Sam said, pausing to face me.

"I should be able to head back in a couple of days," I said as we walked to toward his horse. "I just want to make certain Ivy and Bryn are settled." I stalled a bit, not wanting him to leave.

"Sam, there's something—there's one thing—" I stumbled on my words, knowing what I wanted to say, but not trusting whether I should say it.

Sam waited patiently, maybe enjoying my moment of discomfort.

"I want you to think about joining me…maybe we could consider a home together in Turner Creek?"

Sam's eyebrows lifted.

"Or somewhere else," I quickly added, feeling awkwardly uncertain.

"Hannah. Marie. Wright." Sam took my hands in his. "Are you going to get on one knee and propose to me?"

I realized my suggestion did sound like a marriage proposal. I started to laugh.

"Oh, now marrying me is a joke?" Sam released my hands, pretending to be insulted.

"Truthfully?" he said, lightly kissing the top of my head. "I like the idea of a new place. Together. For us both."

"It does seem like a quick engagement," I teased. "But I think you fancied marrying me when we were kids."

Sam smiled and looked away, shaking his head at the memories ignited by my teasing.

"Was I that obvious?" he asked.

I nodded.

"But I need to be honest… I won't be able to commit to that move right away. Your father gave me a few leads on the traders responsible for Night Star's, Morning Owl's and my father's deaths. Only one of them is still alive, finishing the last of his days in a Montana prison. Plus, I'd like to meet my half-siblings, to learn more about them and…maybe even more about my father."

"How's your mom taking this line of investigation?" I asked cautiously.

"She won't talk about him. She never would. But I need to know more." Sam paused. "I had plenty of men in my life growing up, but I longed for…no, I ached to know what my father was like."

"And so we both carry on. Trusting we will start our life together when we're both ready," I added, knowing it best to finish old business before taking on new.

"Hopefully that happens before Bryn is old enough to marry us!" Sam said, laughing.

"Hopefully that happens after you've moved beyond kissing the top of my head!" I said, knowing he'd been waiting respectfully for some signal to show a deeper kind of affection.

I needed him to know I was ready.

He lowered his lips to mine.

For the first time, I gave and received unconditional, intimate love. It was scary and exhilarating at the same time.

"Until tomorrow." Sam mounted his horse.

"And long after." I blew him a kiss and watched him ride away.

To the Reader

I always study the front and the back matter of a book before reading it. I love to discover who the book is dedicated to, who the author is and how an idea transformed into a book

If you are like me and you are reading this page, I thought you might find it interesting to know the idea for this book emerged in the late 1990s and first took shape as a screenplay. Although I was unsuccessful in marketing and selling this original screenplay, Hannah's story continued to call for my attention.

When I commenced converting my screenplay into a novel, many of the characters and conflicts needed updating. As I updated and wrote, new dimensions emerged, resulting in a better story than the original.

While Hannah was calling me to rewrite her story, Ivy and Thomas were asking me to tell theirs:

The prequel is the story of Ivy and Thomas, called *Confluence*.

The sequel is the story of Bryn's great granddaughter.

HEATHER ROSELLE has entertained thoughts
of being a published writer for much of her adult
life.

She has dabbled in screenwriting, non-fiction
and now, for the first time, fiction.

www.hroselle.ca